PHARRICIDE

VINCENT DE SWARTE

PHARRICIDE

TRANSLATED FROM THE FRENCH
BY NICHOLAS ROYLE

Pharricide first published by Calmann-Lévy in 1998

This translation first published by Cōnfingō Publishing in 2019

249 Burton Road, Didsbury, Manchester, M20 2WA
www.confingopublishing.uk

Pharricide by Vincent de Swarte © Calmann-Lévy, 1998
English translation © Nicholas Royle, 2019

Art Direction & Typesetting by Zoë McLean, zoe@confingopublishing.uk

Printed by TJ International Ltd

A CIP catalogue record for this book is available from the British Library
ISBN 978-0-9955966-2-7

2 4 6 8 10 9 7 5 3 1

For my mother.

Contents

Foreword

The Tour de Cordouan is the oldest lighthouse in France. Construction began in 1548. It is a magnificent conical tower with three galleries, and throughout this most functional of structures there is a profusion of gilt and statuary, stained-glass windows and elegantly arched doorways. At 223 feet, or 68 metres, it has been called the Versailles of the Sea. It is also the setting for a magnificently perverse short novel by Vincent de Swarte, first published in French in 1998. De Swarte died at the age of 42 in 2006. Nicholas Royle has now made a brilliantly lucid, idiomatic translation of de Swarte's masterpiece for English readers.

Narrated in the first person, it takes the form of the journal entries of a strange man called Geoffroy Lefayen, the new keeper of the light. Already there's a good joke at work here, for Geoffroy is himself a keeper of no kind of light, but of a great darkness, rather, that only grows more dense and weird as the story progresses. Best read in one sitting, *Pharricide* has at its core a man in relation to a great structure which he feels has almost entirely overwhelmed him. He writes that Cordouan has 'stripped my soul naked', and more ominously, 'has saved my knives from retirement'.

What is it in the imagination that links the lighthouse to ideas of madness? It is surely solitude, but not solitude alone. For many years there was a regulation in the American Lighthouse Service that no fewer than three keepers can be in residence at any one time. Too often, with only a pair of keepers, one eventually murdered the other. Geoffroy is alone in his tower, but early on will mention that there's been 'the faintest trace of madness in the air'. But he knows his duties, as does Vincent de Swarte, and the reader is never in doubt as to the authenticity of this keeper's daily rounds. We are also reminded of that other element of the story, the sea, with its conger eels and salt water, its buoys and crayfish, high winds and sandbanks and seagulls. And time: 'the hours passing by with the rhythm of a salt-ravaged clock.'

There's something else too. It becomes clear early on that Geoffroy has a taxidermic bent. He likes to stuff dead things. The reader's misgivings about this odd, solitary man are by no means laid to rest with this revelation.

One way of writing madness from a first-person perspective relies on subtlety. The slow, inexorable accumulation of small warps and anomalies arouses unease in the reader, and the horror arrives as a kind of awakening rather than a shock. There is another way, however, the full-on approach: the stick of gelignite to the central nervous system, like the first slurp of a good gin martini. There is a short novel by the great American writer John Hawkes called *Travesty*, which has much in common with *Pharricide*. It begins: 'No, no, Henri. Hands off the wheel. Please. It is too late. After all, at one hundred and forty-nine kilometres per hour on a country road in the darkest quarter of the night, surely it is obvious that your slightest effort to wrench away the wheel will pitch us into the toneless world of highway tragedy even more quickly than I have planned.'

Hard then not to think of Poe, for example the first sentence of *The Cask of Amontillado*: 'The thousand injuries of Fortunato I had borne as I best could, but when he ventured upon insult I vowed revenge.'

Vincent de Swarte is of this school, and his reader is soon in deep water. 'The lighthouse pretty much let me sleep until five,' he writes, and we are aware that this is no mere piece of whimsy. As with Hawkes and Poe, we suspect that with confusions of agency like this, we are entering psychotic territory. Then when visitors arrive, an English couple, we know the story is soon properly to begin, and that de Swarte has thus far only been clearing his throat. And as with Hawkes and Poe, the voice remains calm, cold and clinical throughout. The sentences chill the heart, yet even so, in prose of this calibre, there lies a kind of redemptive power, even if it speaks only of madness and evil; and we read on. There is an entry in Geoffroy's journal hereabouts that ends with his admission that he had 'half-opened the door to a sewer in Hell'.

Nor does this narrator long remain a cipher to us. He understands clearly his apprenticeship in evil, and his induction into a curious school of specialised taxidermic endeavour. In the memoirs of the psycho-analyst Abram Kardiner, who was one of the few who were actually analysed by Freud, the author speaks about his childhood phobia of masks. Freud then tells him that 'the first mask you saw was your dead mother's face'. It occurs to the reader that Geoffroy's own florid symptoms might share a similar aetiology, particularly when he speaks of his 'House of Perfection', by which he means his 'family', which no longer exhibits the messy incoherent vitality of actual living beings.

Not unlike the narrator of Hawkes's *Travesty*, whom we saw driving fast across France at dead of night, with his daughter and her lover helpless passengers, fearing the worst, Geoffroy considers himself an art-ist. He too feels that willed destruction is the ultimate act of the poetic imagination. He is also, he tells us, a *gourmand*. His love of crayfish began with his moth-er, he says. 'Even if I was ill, in the toilet every five minutes, I'd still guzzle them up. I'm made that way. All gourmands are made that way.' It is the vanity of the mad.

Can love have a place in such a story? A woman will come to the lighthouse, Lise, a magnificent, red-haired, hard-drinking creature of large sexual appe-tites. She admires Geoffroy's 'work'. She tells him he is an artist. He writes in his journal: 'It won't be easy to kill her.' As de Swarte engineers a conflation of love and death, or at least the possibility thereof, we realise we are approaching a heart of darkness of which Bataille would have approved. The novel leaps forward with a charged energy that is surely adequate to power it to its climax. There is a superb structural organisation here, even as trouble threatens Geoffroy's paradise. Bizarrely, the reader is rooting for him, rooting for him and his girl, in fact. What a wealth of pathology is here, in this bold, transgressive, brilliantly controlled logbook of the damned!

A comedy ends with a wedding or a party or both. In a black comedy, all that should be white is black, as in a photographic negative. There is a glorious inversion of a wedding party, a perfection of horror, where nadir and acme are as one. Lise, writes our narrator, was happy. 'She didn't even appear to mind the smell.'

Scott Fitzgerald is quoted close to the end of the novel, with a passage in which he describes the mentally ill as 'mere guests on earth, eternal strangers carrying around broken decalogues that they cannot read'. The reader is reminded of Melville's Queequeg, who in the late stages of *Moby-Dick* carves his coffin with the grotesqueries of his own tattoos, which represent an encoded theory of the heavens and the earth, 'a mystical treatise on the art of attaining truth', in Melville's words. The only problem being that Queequeg cannot read it. Nevertheless it is this carved coffin which will save Ishmael, narrator and sole survivor of *Moby-Dick* and Ahab's *Pequod*. It seems entirely appropriate, then, that it is Melville's masterpiece, and Fitzgerald's implicit allusion to it, that lift the final grim pages of this great short tale of the sea.

Patrick McGrath
New York City, November 2018

PHARRICIDE

Cordouan: lighthouse situated in the Gironde estuary, on the island of Antros. White tower with lantern, median section and dark-grey outer wall. Height 64.8 metres above the high seas. Range 21 miles. Latitude: N 45° 35' 11". Longitude: W 1° 10' 25".

3 October

My mother called me Geoffroy, like my elder brother, stillborn a year before me. (My father entered a monastery a month before I was born and has not been heard from since.) I've always been frightened of my Christian name, the very sound of it, and have never liked to hear it combined with my surname, Lefayen. At school, people called me His Lordship, despite the fact my mother kept chickens on the wasteland surrounding our dilapidated 1960s house on the outskirts of Saint-Brieuc. Later, when I was working, I became known as the Egyptian (a reference to my being disinclined to conversation, a trait not particularly unusual, however, among deep-sea fishermen). With hindsight, the nickname was appropriate. It was an omen.

My taciturn character didn't win me a lot of friends. There was Jean Frot, a colleague at Pierres Noires, although we've lost touch. And the two Rogers, on *La Geneviève*, but they ended up in prison, and at the time of writing they must still be there, fifteen years later. Either that or dead. There's also Joël, who likes what I do (he calls me an artist). And that's it, as far back as I can remember.

I don't have much to say, I'm not particularly sociable, but I am, I think, kind. I feel it warming me from inside, this kindness. It feels solid, if naive. Deep down inside me there's this desire to engage in play, like a child, or a dog you might throw a stick for, further and further, who fetches it tirelessly, tail wagging, chops dripping, eyes proud and half-crazed, snout in the air, panting in a panic that the game might end. I'd happily accept being sent back to my kennel with a sharp word or a slap for being a nuisance. That's me, deep down: a big soft doggie. All men, deep down, are just big soft doggies. The problem is it's so deep down they tend to forget it.

Rather than turn into the kind of dog that barks at postmen, and everyone else for that matter, I made the decision to go to sea, and, eight years ago now, to be a lighthouse keeper. It may not always be easy spending week after week on a scrap of an island, your ears full of the sound of the water crashing on the rocks, and nothing much to see apart from your navel or the horizon – each as unattainable as the other. But, remote from mankind, I feel human. My only audience the wind, the seagulls, the crabs, but human all the same – kind, I suppose. Anyway, I don't see what else I could be. Not even a deep-sea fisherman. I could be a hermit, perhaps, looking after three goats on a deserted plateau. A monk, if the Catholics' god were my friend, but the Catholics' god is not my friend. No, really, I don't see what else I could be.

Recently it came to my attention that within Lighthouses and Beacons I'm highly thought of. For my willingness to take risks, my strong constitution and my heroic physique. They say I'll enter the annals. That I stand out, even if the profession isn't short of people like me. A 'magnetic' character, no less, is how one engineer put it.

These kindnesses came my way after the difficulties at Cordouan. The lantern's two thousand watts burnt a hole in Joël's retinas, a thousand watts for each of his drink-sozzled eyes. Misfortune never striking only once, the couple who shared caretaking duties with him died in a road accident eight days later. The administration installed two trainees as a stopgap, but there were problems: stories of smuggling, or something along those lines, they didn't go into detail. And so they thought of me. They said: 'It's not hard work. With the generators, the lighthouse pretty much looks after itself, as you know. Sure, there's the maintenance, perhaps a bit more than elsewhere, in any case more than at Pierres Noires, but it's no big deal. Most important are the six months up to April. All the same, we'll do everything possible to find you a colleague. There's a retired keeper in the area who has volunteered to split the job fifty-fifty. Or there's always trainees. You know what we're going to do? You can do it till Christmas, with supplies arriving every three weeks. Then it's the holiday and in January we'll see where we are. If you feel like it, you sign up again. If not, we'll find someone else. Naturally, you'll be on a bonus.'

And so on. You would have thought they were talking about sending me to the moon. Six months, no big deal. Back in the day, one of my predecessors did two years solo at Eddystone. OK, so afterwards he drank himself to death. But six months is not two years. At Pierres Noires, when Jean Frot and I were stuck without supplies for thirteen weeks, I'd almost say I was unhappy to finally catch sight of the swinging hoist of the supply vessel. I would happily have signed up for three more months, and then three more after that, had it been necessary. Even two years, in spite of the wind that smashes into the windows like a gangster's fist and the water that tumbles down the steps night after night, without which it would just be too easy.

A rarefied life doesn't frighten me.

Only one thing frightens me at Cordouan: my Egyptian magnetism. I pray to God no one comes to the lighthouse during those six months, no one at all, neither the engineer from Lighthouses and Beacons, nor the keeper on the supply vessel. I'll be perfectly happy with fish and crabs until April. Who needs fresh fruit and vegetables? Who needs a Christmas hamper?

10 October

From the coast, Cordouan knocks you for six. Even
on a rainy day, you have a perfect view of the lighthouse. You can almost see the monkey faces, dolphins
and acanthus leaves that decorate the apertures. On
a fine day, it floats on the horizon like a mirage. It
takes no more than an hour by launch from Royan.
I'll never forget, as long as I live, the first reconnais-
sance trip, last month. It was unusually sunny for the
time of year, according to the engineer from Verdon.
I watched my future home advance towards me like a
monitor lizard rising up on its hind legs. I was proud
and anxious at the same time. What madness had
driven someone to chisel away at a stone tower like it
was a chair leg – in the middle of the ocean? And by
what miracle was it still standing, more or less intact,
after four centuries at the mercy of the swell, as majestic as ever? The tourist brochures call it the 'king

of lighthouses'. Absolutely right: it makes you want to get down on your knees and whisper words of respect or prayer. A king of Atlantis. Like a submarine surfacing, at speed, tearing through the water, and now there it is, self-assured, relaxed, looking out for ships almost with nonchalance, aloof, taunting us with its superiority.

We beached at seven in the morning. The water was clear as glass. Golden sand crunched under our feet. Accompanied by a colony of herring gulls we waited a good half-hour for the tide to go out completely, then we got our boots wet as we made our way to the postern, where the trainee lighthouse keepers were waiting for us. I requested a tour of the structure: the protective outer ring enclosing the kitchen, the bedrooms, the engineer's room (formerly the apartments of the king's lieutenant), the radio and the generators. Then vertically, from the cellars to the very lenses of the lantern. Two hundred and ninety steps lead to the chapel and the three rooms beneath the watch room. Finally, the gallery, like the roof of the world, with no function during the day, apart from to remind you how small you are, that you're prone to vertigo, sore throats, conjunctivitis, even madness. Otherwise, there's much to admire. The emptiness, all around. Or, at low tide on the Pointe de Grave side, the astonishing beach of Cordouan like a truncated whale's tail. And if you lean out, still at low tide but on the rocky side, the giant shadow of the lighthouse pointing towards where the dangerous currents lie.

We ate in the lighthouse. The trainees seemed happy, even if I was far from the ideal guest; the engineer talked enough for two. Then we made an inventory of the various jobs. I surprised everybody by needing no more than a couple of hours to complete that task. From the professional's point of view, nothing resembles a lighthouse so much as another lighthouse, as long as they use the same system. Apart from that it just comes down to different ways of getting bored. The trainees showed me a couple of good spots for fishing, and the best hiding places for crabs, the rocks with the best supplies of mussels, and the best holes for prawns. All that remained to do after that was have a drink.

The launch, *La Pibale*, arrived with the next ebb tide. We got wet again, up to our thighs, and my lighthouse slowly moved away from me, fading like a photograph of a forgotten woman as the light drained from the sky. I didn't take my eyes from it until we reached land.

At that time, I still hadn't given a definitive response to the Administration. When I saw Cordouan emit its first blasts of light – green, white and red – into the night as the watch started, I remember experiencing a moment of hesitation. However, apart from my 'good morning' on our arrival, a few banalities and two or three questions about procedure, these were the only words the engineer heard from my lips during the whole of that mesmerising day: 'I'll do it. Without a colleague. Without trainees. And without the old man.'

14 October

I feel amazing, a new experience for me. As a result, I want to please people, also a new experience. Shame there's no one around to share my excitement with. This lighthouse, this beautiful lighthouse, has entered me and every one of its white stones is turning me white, too, from the inside out. I feel I'm becoming the lighthouse. I'm lighting up. Last month, when I first set eyes on it, love at first sight...

Even though it's hardly my specialist subject, it's definitely love. Well, my idea of love anyway. The idea of being the other, the feeling of belonging, giving yourself over.

The other, for me, is the lighthouse.

Cordouan has woken me up. Cordouan has stripped my soul naked. It has reminded me of everything that lies within. It has replaced maybe with definitely.

I always had a vague feeling this day would come. I just didn't know when.

It turns out to be today. Cordouan has saved my knives from retirement.

15 October

My days ring as hollow as empty shells. In the morning I turn off the light a quarter of an hour before sunrise. I go up to check, pointlessly perhaps, and make my first radio transmission of the day. After that, I have time to kill. I sink the net at half-tide and pull it up three hours later hoping to find something better than gobies and seaweed. I polish the banister and the ironwork up in the gallery, clean the glass of the lantern till it shines, brush the floor of the watch room, maintain the door frames, repair an electric wire in the upper stairway, oil the hinges. Basically, I do odd jobs to kill time. At eleven o'clock I start to prepare lunch and at midday sit down to eat. From one till four I potter about, watch a bit of TV, make the bed or play patience, do a crossword, give the rowing boat a lick of paint, tighten a screw on the fuel tank, check the pipes on the rainwater tanks, pace the foreshore in my waders, scrub mussels for dinner, look after my crayfish farm, which goes with me everywhere, like a woman's make-up bag (I love crayfish), climb up to the gallery to kill half an hour – there's always that. At five o'clock I make the second radio transmission. I switch on the light a quarter of an hour before sunset, and I go up to check, although I still don't really need to, but while I'm there I can check the buoys in the vicinity and the other lighthouses within range. If there's a problem, which is unusual, I call La Coubre or Terre-Nègre, and if either of them confirms that something is up, I call the subdivision. I eat in front of the TV, wash up, go round with the brush or floor cloth, carry on watching TV in my bedroom. I fill in the log sometimes while watching, sometimes after, and write in my diary always after. I doze until one o'clock, the time we would change watch if there were two of us, climb up to the light, counting the steps, come back down counting them again, and go back to bed until sunrise.

Just a quick sketch of a random day, the hours passing by with the rhythm of a salt-ravaged clock. Since yesterday, however, there's been the faintest trace of madness in the air. I've been checking my knives and equipment. The prospect of getting down to work makes me mad with joy.

21 October

Two days ago I caught a young conger eel from the rocks, taking care to cause as little damage as possible to its gleaming skin as I landed it. After it had spent a day in the freezer, I washed it and placed it on a sheet. Then, for some time, I stroked it. It's not strictly necessary for what comes next, but this beautiful creature is dead, so the least I can do is offer a little consolation. 'Little conger,' I whispered, 'cut down in your prime, you'll ascend to conger heaven, in the great celestial sea, where no doubt your parents and friends will be waiting for you. You're not going to turn up all ruffled, dirty, out of sorts and poorly. I've got to make you look good, prepare you, adorn you, make you up like you were when you were alive, better even. I'll try to make you look even better. Relax, you're in good hands, the hands of Uncle Geoffroy, friend to congers and to all fish in all the seas.' Words of reassurance to any creature in serious difficulty.

On the mahogany table in the engineer's room I arranged, on the left, my knives, needles, pins, tweezers, scissors, brushes and glass eyes (I like to see the eyes right from the start, even if they are the final touch of the work, just because they're pretty, a spray of eyes on brass stems), and, on the right, the borax, a reel of thread, nails, tacks, wax, glue, finishing powders, and, in the middle, the large tools. I bent over my baby conger and made a clean cut from the head to the tail along the flank where I'd inserted the gaff to land it. I cut the fins, severed the bones from the head and gills, separated the skin from the body, excavated the eyes, removed the tongue, scraped away the flesh, removed the cheeks, washed the skin and sprinkled with borax. Next, in place of the flesh and entrails, I inserted a new plaster body that will never rot. It was like transplanting eternity, casting reinforced concrete that will last for centuries upon centuries, bestowing eternal life. I pampered a little more with the powder, before stitching the skin with rot-proof thread.

I thought again of the two Rogers. Of their religious silence during operations, the kind of silence that accompanies delicate handiwork. Nothing could have distracted them, neither a big wave, nor even a worrying pitch or roll. *La Geneviève* could have sunk straight to the bottom of the sea without them lifting their heads.

I'll get back to work on the conger in a few days. I'll pull back the pieces of card holding the fins in place, choose a glass eye after trying several, an eye that pleases me, not necessarily one that looks exactly like the real eye. I'll place a stick in its mouth, spray it pearly grey and mount it on an oval-shaped piece of varnished wood with chiselled grooves. I'll finish it off good and proper. All that will be left to do after that will be to find a wall good enough for it. Such walls are not in short supply at Cordouan. Perhaps above the postern to welcome visitors. Or in the watch room. I also thought about the chapel, but, if I'm honest, the idea made my blood run cold.

Although at the moment it's still covered in hair slides, something tells me that out of my entire career as an amateur taxidermist the conger eel from the island of Antros will end up being my most beautiful piece. OK, I'm getting carried away because it's been a long time… But it has a good chance. If Joël Lacassanne could see it, he'd be speechless. The man who spent the long hours stolen off him by various lighthouses constructing miniature merry-go-rounds for his poor little retard of a son – Damien – would say: 'No doubt about it, Geoffroy, you're an artist.' And deep down inside, where I feel that kindness, I'd be happy.

Lights out. It's gone two. Never mind that this baby conger eel will eat into my sleep. If I really can't get to sleep, I'll climb up to the lantern. No doubt there'll be a seagull up there to chat to for five minutes.

26 October

Apart from the daily routine, I've passed the last few days bent over my conger eel, until yesterday, Wednesday, when the supply boat turned up forty-eight hours ahead of schedule on account of the gales they've been forecasting since Friday. I told them on the phone that it could wait, but they didn't want to know. The guy was being all matey. I couldn't work out why.

— I'll stay in the watch room.

— Something wrong, Lefayen?

— No, everything's fine. But I'd rather not see you, you know. It's easier if I don't see anyone. I've already got a ton of overtime compared to normal. I've got to get into the zone for winter. If I see someone, I won't be able to get into the zone. Next month, I'll be in the zone, it won't matter if I see anyone or not. But at the moment I'm shutting myself away, trying to get into the zone. Seeing you will do me more harm than good.

— When the engineer comes, you'll have to show yourself.

— Yeah, well, I'll manage. That's different. He's connected with the lighthouse, whereas you guys are all about dry land, everything cosy. Your houses, your wives. It'll wind me up if I see you, doesn't matter whether you're coming or going.

— Anything special you need?

— If you could get hold of some rock salt. Ten-kilo bags. A few of them.

— That's a lot of salt.

— It's for the fish. For my taxidermy. Garlic as well, just a few heads. That's for the crayfish. They go really well together in the oven. And a lock. There's a problem with a lock in the lamp room.

The salt just came to me while we were talking. I've got some at the lighthouse, but I might run out. As for the rest, I was lying, of course, with all that talk about getting used to solitude. If I prefer to see no one, it's because I'm afraid I'll fail to be reasonable. Afraid I'll be tempted. Afraid of that fear of myself that I've already spoken about. And I did terribly well to double-lock the door to the watch room and chuck the key out of the window when they arrived, because Cordouan had been doing my head in since dawn. It had been driving me mad. I'd been sweating like never before and hurting everywhere, deep in my bones, seeing images of rotting carcasses passing before my eyes, hearing the screeching sirens of a lightship. I'd had to gag myself to avoid howling, banging my head against a wardrobe, although not before, by some random flash of lucidity, placing a blanket between my head and said item of furniture, and piercing my forearms with sharp, precise jabs from my number three knife, number ten blade, before ending up crouching in my own piss, crying out like an epileptic conger eel. That lasted… I don't know. An hour, two hours. I lost kilos, I lost salt. I lost the plot. And then from a great distance I heard the sound of voices and laughter, which told me that down below they had heard nothing. When one of the men came up to tell me they were leaving, I was able to murmur my thanks through the door. The engine of *La Pibale* reminded me of that of *La Geneviève*, and I stayed until the evening blubbing like a woman on the bed in the watch room holding a threadbare one-eyed teddy bear tightly enough to suffocate the poor thing.

30 October

The night did me some good. The lighthouse pretty much let me sleep until five. I had a hot shower, like you might do when you get cold, and disinfected my forearms.

I've never had such a violent fit. The last one was fifteen years ago, on *La Geneviève*, where I stayed in the toilet the whole afternoon, during which I must have thrown up every fifteen minutes, and not on account of the sea.

The shower repaired me, cured me. The skin on my forearms is growing back before my eyes. By tomorrow you wouldn't know there'd been anything wrong, or perhaps the day after tomorrow. I feel cheerful, lighthearted. I feel like bursting out laughing. I'm full of love. I want to kiss the rocks, the silt, the crabs, the seagulls, my crayfish and the whole world.

Having changed the lock on the watch room door that I'd had to force yesterday in order to gain exit, I felt an enormous sense of achievement: I successfully hung up my little conger eel in the chapel, in place of the crucifix, which I chucked into the oculus, as if it were a waste-disposal chute.

2 November

The wind has been trying to unscrew the lighthouse
since this morning. The waves are in the grip of the
moon, throwing themselves at the rocks, and the rain
has been relentlessly, hatefully reducing the sand on
the beach to a series of furrows. So I'm watching
more TV than usual. This afternoon I watched one
natural history documentary after another. The first
one was about a strange sickness that can bring a lion
to its knees in minutes. I should have changed chan-
nel. Seeing pictures of these majestic big cats in such
agony shocked me more than I would have thought
possible. Throughout life we are assailed by images,
not only on TV, that grate against us, even destroy
us. We believe we're so strong. We make a joke of
things. That lion was stopped in its tracks, as if its
adductors had snapped, just like that. Then it was
seized by terrible convulsions. Even its jaw was trem-

bling. Lying down on its side this magnificent beast was reduced to a toy with a flat battery. It breathed in with difficulty, as if its nostrils had been packed with cotton wool. You could already see in its eyes a look of resignation, the resignation of a senior combatant choosing not to put up a fight against a stronger opponent. After several increasingly painful breaths, in a fraction of a second it was as if this great animal had been run over by a truck or shot with a rifle at close range. Its huge head fell to one side and it gave a final wheezy exhalation, like a set of discarded bagpipes.

The second documentary outdid the first in terms of violence. It was a Cousteau film about the tropical cousins of the fish in the estuary. We've seen them a thousand times on TV, these multicoloured fish with their silly names brushing past divers in their worryingly aquarium-like sea. But the dormant taxidermist inside me was awakened once more. I am, after all, hypersensitive. My knives can feel. I'm a full-time artist. How good one of those would look above the postern. The Picasso triggerfish, for example. Or, better still, the angelfish. Yes, the angelfish. It would announce the philosophy of this place in poetic fashion. One look and you'd sense that if you stuff a living creature, death is not the end, whether it's a conger eel, a lion, or even you or me.

6 November

The English couple arrived this morning. When they phoned me last week, I did nothing to encourage or discourage them. I simply said OK. We agreed on the day and yesterday I went fishing. I caught a four-pound bass.

The Englishwoman is very English. Well, according to the idea that I have of the English. Her skin is pale, paler than I've hardly ever seen. She has unusually dark circles under her eyes and her hair is dyed black, which accentuates the waxy pallor of her face. But she has beautiful forearms, well-defined muscles, with beautiful, transparent bluish veins. She wears exactly the kind of jumper I like on a woman: V-necked and angled away from the body by breasts that are big and yet pointed at the same time. Her neck is appetising, streaked with natural necklaces, like she has just woken up. Her hands are long but not thin. However, even though she's wearing trousers, I'm sure she doesn't have beautiful legs. You can see it in her eyes. Women who have lovely legs, they let you know it even when they're wearing trousers (I read that one day in a book and I liked it).

He's very English, too. He has red hair and that particular kind of pale skin you get with red hair. He's rather tall and well built. He has class and is well turned out, decked out in expensive yachtie gear, like the filthy rich of Noirmoutier. What I liked immediately about him was his kindness, because it reminded me of my own, which resides deep down inside me. But he knows how to show his and express it, probably because he's with a woman. He has a great smile, too, matching his kindness, exactly the kind of smile that I have never known how to do, the smile of people who are flourishing and have better things to do with their life than be a lighthouse keeper.

Standing before the lighthouse, they both rolled their eyes in the same way, part wonder, part respect, as I must surely have done two months ago.

I insisted they stay for lunch. As we ate, they asked me all the questions that tourists ask a lighthouse keeper, mostly him because he spoke better than her, and I replied with a degree of ease and indulgence that surprised me at the time. But in retrospect, I know why I was in such a good mood.

The Englishman explained that he also held French nationality and that as a child he used to come on family holidays to Royan. He was kind of in love with the lighthouse, he said. Since he was very little, he had promised himself that he would one day marry the love of his life in the lighthouse. The Englishwoman turned scarlet at this. So did I, for that matter. They didn't yet have the priest's authorisation, but they were confident. They knew that there had recently been baptisms performed in the lighthouse. They were thinking about the first few days of nice weather, just before the tourist season.

On the phone last week, when they talked about their plans to get married, it seemed to me a magnificent idea, marrying a woman here, in this round chapel where, long ago, there'd been a bust of Louis XIV. That evening, I became morose and knelt on a prie-dieu with, in my left hand, an imaginary hand, that of my imaginary wife, often to be found by my side as I go to sleep, even if I can't put a name or a face to her. Everyone was there from my circle: Joël, his wife and Damien, Jean Frot, Monsieur Rouleau (who looked after me after my mother was sectioned, more like a mug than a man), my brother Geoffroy, the two Rogers, my mother and even my father, who I know to be still alive and living not far away.

Too bad if three-quarters of them are undesirable. At least they made up the numbers.

That evening at Cordouan there was a little love in everyone's heart.

After lunch, the English couple accompanied me to the end of the beach, the bit that's like a truncated whale's tail. I had two stakes to drive into the wet sand there.

I waved away their questions, telling them they were mooring posts for the flat-bottomed boat. These explanations seemed to suffice, which was convenient as I would have been a bit stuck if, incredulous, they had asked, 'Mooring posts? In the sand? With the tide?'

He helped me, while she devoured her future husband with her eyes.

It was particularly mild. Inspired more by her buoyant mood than by the slack water of the middle of the day, she said, with a heavy accent:

— I want to swim.

— Put one toe in the water and you'll change your mind. It's freezing, Katleen. Am I not right, Geoffroy?

Steeven was holding on to the steps I was standing on to bang in the stakes.

— Definitely. Although there is a warm current at low tide, no more than five metres out. It's possible to swim, even at this time of year.

— Really?

They were so wrapped up in each other they would have believed anything.

At the moment, they are visiting the chapel.

I can hear them laughing. If I lean over the oculus, I can even see them.

They are hand in hand. Very much in love.

This is what I said just before our walk on the beach this afternoon: 'I've got a four-pound bass in the fridge and a bottle of Graves. There's no shortage of rooms here. There are five empty bedrooms in the lower ring. It's romantic here in the evening. You have to experience Cordouan by night. Everyone should spend a night at Cordouan.'

7 November

My bass was a success. We had a great evening. He was so funny. She was a little drunk, enough to believe herself bilingual.

— *Vous devez bien connaître vous-même, mister Geoffroy, avec un job pareil. Et quel courage! Moi qui souis mort de peur quand je souis là où le roi va que tout'seule…*

Katleen collapsed in a cascade of laughter that reverberated all the way up to the lantern.

— *C'est bien ainsi qu'on dit, mister Steeven Seltzner,* my sweet teacher.

The 'sweet teacher' held in his hairy hands the second bottle of Graves, which I had just opened. He kept offering to pour me a glass, but each time I refused.

Towards ten o'clock, the engaged couple were sufficiently drunk to judge as sensible my suggestion that we should go and check that the tide had not carried off the two stakes on the beach. Even if the Englishwoman would actually have preferred to go up and have a look at the lantern.

— Afterwards, I said.

— *Bien mon capitaine*, she intoned, pretending to stand to attention.

I recommended a jumper, jacket, boots and a hat. It had been a nice day, but at this time of year the sea reclaims the island from late afternoon.

The English couple didn't mention my shoulder bag. They negotiated the channels with the aid of a torch, which was more or less redundant on account of the moon. From time to time, Steeven shone it at the sea or amused himself by covering and uncovering the beam.

— *Secteur rouge, danger*, he yelled.

We reached the sand and walked for a few minutes in silence until the Englishwoman complained of being cold. Her intended draped his jacket about her shoulders.

— *On y est*, mister Geoffroy?

Steeven was perhaps concerned by the sustained pace I was setting.

It was my turn to switch on a torch and I shone it right in his face. I could clearly see that he was beginning to appreciate the absurdity of our presence on a Cordouan sandbank at ten o'clock in the evening with the temperature now below zero. In other words, the cold air had sobered him up. He issued a command.

— *On rentre.*

Katleen was in agreement.

— *Oui, on rentre. J'ai froid.*

Steeven looked at my shoulder bag.

— *Vous avez quoi, là-dedans?*

We were about a hundred metres from the two stakes, which we could see fairly clearly. A pair of sea-gulls perched on them, making them seem like there was some point to them. I don't know why, but at that moment the stakes made me think of the two common criminals either side of Christ.

— In here? Some rope, I said.

And, because I sensed that if I waited I risked losing the upper hand, I rushed Steeven and punched him in the Adam's apple, which first caused him to choke, then to become unsteady on his feet while his wife-to-be dashed towards the lighthouse screaming like a madwoman. I caught her and found a way to calm her down as well. I muzzled her to stop her bawling, tied her hands behind her back and blindfolded her.

Steeven lay on the sand, semi-conscious. I quickly tied him up, then dragged my two bundles towards the stakes looking out to sea.

The seagulls had moved away to the left and been joined by a few others.

The Englishwoman was crying, jolts running through her body. He was crying as well. In that moment, having failed to blindfold him, I happened to catch his eye. He gave me a searching look, as if he wanted, not an explanation exactly, but to know if there might still be a way out. Events had taken hold of me to the extent that I could hardly breathe. It was as if I had been taken over by my actions. My chest had expanded, my brain was full, my entire being was focused on what I was doing. Steeven could see it in my eyes and his questions disappeared from his own. He turned to look at the woman he had expected to marry, but, as if to avoid further suffering, he didn't look at her for very long.

They had already wet themselves, and the rest. What else could they do? Understand? Was I going to burden them with problems that did not concern them and that in any case they would not have been able to resolve?

I tied them to the stakes, facing the lighthouse, and removed the blindfold from the Englishwoman. Her eyes were mad with fear. They found those of her beloved, where, presumably, she would normally find reassurance.

Quite quickly, however, she ceased to struggle. She allowed her head to fall on to her shoulder, her eyes now blank. She reminded me of the lion from the documentary. I'd be ready to believe she felt a sense of relief. I liked that lucidity. Consequently, although I had prepared a sermon on beauty, the purifying sea and their henceforth eternal love, I spared them this extra torture.

Even if on this side of the sandbank the rocks and channels kept any boats at bay, I enveloped the couple in plastic sheeting in which I cut eye and nose holes. I took out a missal and married them at Cordouan, since that had been their wish, promising them to do everything in my power to assure them eternal life.

In less than half an hour, the sea would begin to take care of them. The last image they would take away from this world would be that of the lighthouse, the very image of beauty. Exactly the same image I would like to take away when my day comes. I would not have granted that favour to just anybody.

There was no reason to remain in their company. The great mass of the lighthouse wrapped me in its blackness, while death retreated gradually. It was almost sweet, almost impossible, almost an idea in poor taste. For years I had felt this degree of effort or organisation to be beyond me, but at that precise moment I didn't feel in the slightest bit different from yesterday. Why should I now deserve to go to prison any more than I did yesterday?

However, as I approached my new accomplice, it was anxiety, rather than the wind, that made my hair stand on end. I couldn't stop myself reproaching it, this great stone lizard: 'You see what you've done. You see what you've done to me. You see what you've done to them.'

I turned around one last time. I was a bit far away to be absolutely sure, but it looked like the seagulls had resumed their look-out positions on the two stakes.

This vision calmed me. I walked with a more determined step on the stone paving leading to the lighthouse, even if I sensed deep down that I had just half-opened the door to a sewer in Hell.

8 November

I had some jobs to do early this morning before sunrise. I unmoored the boat belonging to the English couple and took it out to untie the bodies. Seaweed had provided them with attractive wigs. I expected them to be bloated, but they were not. I expelled the seawater they'd swallowed and loaded them on to my wheelbarrow, next to the stakes, which I'd pulled free from the sand. Once I got them back to the lighthouse, I undressed them and washed them carefully. I burned their clothes and stored the bodies in one of the vaulted cellars beneath a thick layer of salt, which will do for now.

Next I went fishing and caught a large mullet. That was lucky, as I felt like cooking properly and mullet needs proper cooking, or it's too bland. There's always the option of barbecuing, but it was drizzling. I washed the mullet, gutted and descaled it, and lay it in a casserole dish on a bed of potatoes and onions. I stuffed it with all the spices I could lay my hands on, especially nutmeg. I love nutmeg with fish. Salt, pepper and a good slosh of the Graves from the night before. At that moment I think I had a hallucination. It seemed to me that, with a spurt of wine, the fish came back to life. So, I didn't hold back. I tipped the rest of the bottle over it. Its mouth half-opened, I'd swear. I uncorked a second bottle and poured and poured, feeding the insane wish that my mullet would recover the use of its muscles and leap, by some miracle, back into the sea. But it didn't move again, not even a quiver of a fin, and while the wine formed a lake at my feet, I took the creature by its tail and beat it against the dish like a temperamental child might have done with its spoon faced with a bowl of mashed carrots. I beat it ten times at least and bawled into the dead air between us, 'Are you going to live? Yes or no? Are you going to live?' But as I had nothing else to threaten it with, I ended up calming down and cleaned the floor. I put the mullet in a hot oven for twenty-five minutes and then ate it.

17 November

The two Rogers – as if having twins wasn't good enough
for their parents, they also gave them the same Christian
name – stuck initially to the world of their studies (one
was a surgeon, the other an archaeologist) and would
later follow in the footsteps of their father, a big shot in
the French Institute of Embalming. No one ever knew
why they abandoned their steady careers for the world
of deep-sea fishing, and still less why, after several years
of perfectly respectable activity, they transformed their
boat into a veritable floating necropolis. No one could
have denied, however, that while fishing off the coast of
Sicily they were gripped by murderous insanity. As irra-
tional as it may seem, I owe my status as the crew's sole
survivor to my physical and psychological qualities and
my culinary talents: they judged me most apt to assist
them, not only by being in charge of supplies but also in
their morbid task.

In the course of one long month, I was witness to funeral ceremonies beyond imagination. The two Rogers practised on their five victims one of the strangest forms of embalming, mixing modern techniques (they had got hold of some Thanatyl, among other fluids, from certain corrupt laboratories) with ancient Chinese, Etruscan and Egyptian practices. I learnt, therefore, first of all under duress and then increasingly willingly, a foul-smelling science that mixed formalin with palm oil. I learnt how to make an incision in a cadaver, either from the pubic bone to the hip, or on the side of the abdomen, according to the whims of the two brothers, and how to treat the blood vessels and the cavities in order to render them as stable as a precious metal. I proved very skilful at removing the brain through the nasal cavities, and not at all clumsy when it came to inserting fine films of linen under the skin. I never balked at handling hunched-up bodies, covering them with bandages before coating them in plaster. I became an expert in the remodelling of features, sinking the eyes to the back of the sockets, placing shells under the eyelids, and painting the faces with various resins. In no time at all, the pupil came to be as skilled as his masters.

I could have killed them both, with the back of my hand. But, strongman though I am, I'd rather allow myself to be led. Twist me around your little finger. I'm basically a dog rolling around in fresh shit. The last week, the two brothers didn't even lock me in my cabin at night. The radio was sitting there. I could have used it. We were practically friends.

No doubt witnessing and learning about these

practices unearthed something deep down that had been waiting to be uncovered, that same something that I felt two months ago when I first set foot on the beach at Cordouan. Even if I had never crossed paths with the two Rogers, I am not convinced that my English couple, at the time of writing, would be sleeping anywhere other than eviscerated in a solution of salt and natron. Perhaps I saved my skin by being the twins' accomplice (they absolved me even before the trial, proof of their mysterious gratitude towards me), but I didn't save my soul, for it was already lost.

The two Rogers never satisfied the curiosity of the judges, the police and the psychiatrists. Even if there may be a thousand explanations, it's a clever man who really understands the horror of humanity. Being on board *La Geneviève*, my veins were infused night and day: the mummies were so realistic you'd believe they could talk. So, thank you to the two Rogers for sticking the mask of the Egyptian jackal on my muzzle, even if it remained hidden away in the shadows of their boat of the dead for more than ten years. There's no doubt it was a master of ceremony who this morning emptied the bodies of Katleen and Steeven, taking care to leave the hearts (we'll understand why). It's definitely a master of ceremony who, as soon as the bicarbonate, sulphate and chloride have taken effect, will transport the desiccated lovers beneath the lantern of the most beautiful of lighthouses, into the watch room transformed for the occasion into the House of Perfection, and cram them full of sawdust, Cordouan sand and synthetic resin. It's a master of ceremony who will coat them in oils, spices, salt, milk and wine, so that their skin becomes as supple as a newborn baby's. It will be a master of ceremony who will seal the incisions in their flanks with wax, unless he hides them behind pretty shells. And, moreover, it's a master of ceremony who, as I have been doing for three weeks now, will set magnificent eyes in re-vivified faces and little golden tongues in mouths that will henceforth be able to utter an eternal 'Yes'.

19 November

The supply boat arrived this morning. This time I behaved.

The guys were reassured to see me. Joël was with them. He looked in a bad way.

We were by the crayfish.

— What do they eat?

— Guts and fish heads. Velvet crabs, prawns, mussels.

— They'll taste pretty salty.

Joël filled his pipe clumsily, then spoke again.

— I get up every night to check the light is lit.

— Tell me about it.

— Too bad I can't see anything.

He was wearing his thick, dark glasses, through which he claimed to be able to make out shapes and even certain colours.

— I wake up my wife. She tells me it's lit. Huh. Like she bothers to check.

— It's lit, Joël. Every night.

— I can't help myself. I bought a telescope. Professional standard. You can count the craters on the moon with it. Or so Damien told me. He's my eyes. I watch the lighthouse with him. He sees it so clearly it's like he's there. He tells me all about it. He saw you once.

The hairs on my arms stood on end and I bit my lip, hard.

— He saw me?

But two of the supplies guys turned up.

— You'll have to have a look in the second cellar, the one that's locked. It doesn't smell too good.

Joël said:

— It'll be saltpetre. You'd better check the tank's not leaking from above. That happened to me.

— Doesn't smell of saltpetre, said one of the men.

— It's my fish, I said. It's my fish drying – it's the products.

A smile alighted on Joël's lips. Possibly it reached his eyes.

— No kidding, Geoffroy. You're back on that?

I didn't reply.

— What kind of fish, Geoffroy?

— Tell you later.

— Why don't you dry them in the open air, under the awning? Or up top, the gallery? It wouldn't stink out the interior.

— That's not the way to do it. They'd go off. Tell you what, let's have a look in the chapel.

We climbed slowly. Once there, I took my conger eel down off the wall and placed it in Joël's hands.

— No kidding! You're at it again.

I smiled. Joël touched the fish with his fingertips, as he must sometimes touch his wife. And then he stretched his arms out as if that would help him see better.

— There's no doubt about it, Geoffroy. You're an artist.

I felt suddenly happy.

— You still see a bit?

— Of course I can see. My fingers can see. And now, I feel. I can feel that you've done a good job. You really are an artist.

— Nah…

— You should teach me.

— I would have taught you, Joël. I would have taught you.

— In another life.

— I'll do you one. And one for your son.

Joël drew on his pipe.

— I'll take it next time we come in the supply boat. He'll be pleased.

— So you reckon he saw me?

— Yes, well, I say he saw you… Although, having said that, Damien has got eyes like a hawk.

— With the telescope?

— Yes.

— That's funny, that.

— Yes, it's funny.

— So when did he see me?

— The other night when there was a new moon. It was really clear, apparently. He saw people on the beach. You know what? Maybe it wasn't you.

I could feel sweat trickling down my sides like crawling insects.

— People? Wasn't me. I haven't seen a soul for six weeks.

— Three people.

— Three?

— Yes. They might even have been fighting.

— Surely I'd have heard them?

— I don't know, Geoffroy. Maybe the wind was blowing in the wrong direction.

— What else?

— They went round to the Gros Terrien bank side and Damien couldn't see them any more.

— Three, you say.

— Yes, three. And a boat that was no longer there in the morning.

— A sailing boat?

— No.

— Maybe that's what I heard around two o'clock.

— That's not possible. They couldn't have stayed until two o'clock because of the tide.

I felt myself going red. I thought even Joël would be able to see it.

— You're right. They must have left earlier. If I'm honest I was watching TV.

— That's happened to me as well, not hearing a boat over the sound of the TV.

— I'll put it down in the log all the same. Just like that, how you told it to me. I'll say I didn't hear anything and that it's thanks to Damien's telescope we've got anything at all. Too bad if they give me a hard time. Anyway, they won't.

— I'm sure they won't give you a hard time. You're doing them a favour. I don't know who would have done it apart from you.

This development has disturbed me greatly. OK, so Joël is a notorious drunk and the testimony of a retard isn't worth shit. All the same, it's worrying.

I could have killed Joël on the steps. It would have been the easiest thing in the world. A bad fall, which everyone would have put down to his failing eyesight. But that would have just made things worse.

I'm wasting my breath. I couldn't raise my hand against Joël.

It's his cretin of a son who deserves to be killed, with a whack from his telescope. That'd teach him not to stick his nose in other people's business.

At four o'clock, when they left, I was very agitated. I was cross with myself for being taken by surprise, for having said some stupid things, for stammering. I'm sure Joël must suspect something. He knows very well that even with the TV on you can hear a boat's engine, especially when the sea is calm, as it was that night.

I still don't know if I should write anything in the log. I just don't know.

This evening the lighthouse is beating at my temples like when they came with the first lot of supplies. It's all Joël's son's fault. He'd better not come prowling around here.

I want to scream. Well, there's nothing stopping me. My one-eyed teddy bear is giving me dirty looks, sad to see his daddy so tired. He'll come and console me and we'll snuggle up in bed together, just like I imagine thousands of couples all over the world are doing right this very moment. It's a nice thought, soothes my heart.

Or I might just go and do some more work in the cellar. That would help me relax.

21 November

I've good reason to love crayfish: my mother bought them whenever she had two pennies to rub together. It's a very happy childhood memory, perhaps my favourite. We went to the market together and I carried them home. I can still hear the slow, languorous sounds the little creatures made as they moved around in the plastic bag. I was less enthusiastic about my mother preparing them for Monsieur Rouleau. He gobbled up half my portion, the bastard. He said they weren't for children, that they would give me an itchy bum. But my mother always put me a few aside in a hiding place for the following day.

It's funny how just after the call from the police I had the crazy notion to get out my cast-iron casserole, the one I use for crayfish. I fished out two kilos of decent specimens. They come from a crayfish farm in Eastern Europe, where they crossbreed them with lobster. The biggest are the size of my hand. They shimmer with a pale jade green and gleaming cobalt blue. I stuck them in a plastic bag that I placed on the kitchen table and listened to them for ages, hypnotised by this slow suffocation of little lives. I must have stayed there at least an hour, sitting on my stool, my chin resting on my hands, like a child with a music box.

I chucked them in the casserole and drizzled the necessary over them. They don't like pepper. With each grind of the mill, they clench up and close ranks, or they get all excited within their armour-plating. They're no keener on oil. Garlic, lots of garlic now they're turning red. A final trickle of oil right at the end, a drop of the hard stuff and a match. Time to eat.

I didn't hold back, but ate everything, right down to their legs, the heads and the roe. I polished off two kilos in no time: Old Man Rouleau can fuck right off.

22 November

— We recovered an inboard Janneau registered ARC 376543 last Tuesday two hundred metres out of Verdon port. Owner Steeven Seltzner was reported missing the evening of 5 November along with his fiancée Katleen Maureen.

On the phone, the cop had a cop's voice. I said that the English couple had called me on 31 October asking to visit the lighthouse, but that they had not turned up. Then I mentioned the brawl that Damien had reported seeing through his telescope, specifying that I had not heard a thing.

— If that was the English couple that night, there must have been a third person on board. What was the date? Sorry, I didn't write it down.

I repeated the date, after which they asked me some more questions like typical police. They wanted to know the exact time the English couple phoned, the day they had wanted to come to the lighthouse, exactly what they'd said on the phone, if I had not been surprised not to see them, et cetera.

Perhaps I should have said that the English couple had come, not stayed very long, and then left. I don't know. I hadn't had time to prepare.

If the cops make enquiries about me with the subdivision, they'll only hear good things.

I don't imagine they'll go back as far as the two Rogers.

However, sooner or later, they're bound to want to come and check out the island. Still, there's no need to think about that.

27 November

I felt quite serene when I heard that the engineer from Lighthouses and Beacons was coming, because I know I'm going to kill him.

I'm no longer setting myself boundaries.

OK, so I've got a telescope being trained on me by a retard, and the police have known of my existence for a week now. But I am at Cordouan and nothing and no one can stop me.

Anyway, the die has been cast. I imagine, if I'd had money, lots of money, I would still have lived my life in the red. Instead of applying the brakes at every warning letter from the bank, I would have doubled my expenditure until they took away my banking privileges. It's like the crayfish. Even if I was ill, in the toilet every five minutes, I'd still guzzle them up. I'm made that way. All gourmands are made that way.

28 November

I had a nice surprise when welcoming the engineer this morning. It's not the bloke I spoke to on the radio, but a woman. A beautiful woman of about forty, red-head, like Steeven but more so.

For the twenty-five metres that separated the launch from the beach, one of the men carried her in his arms.

On the beach, she removed her heels and put on a pair of boots. She looked at her watch and the launch moved away.

Once at the lighthouse she took off her boots and put her heels back on. She has lovely legs and fine ankles, almost too fine. I noticed a little plaster above the heel, under her tights.

She removed one of her pearl-grey leather gloves, men's gloves, and offered me her hand. The nails had had a fresh coat of dark-red nail varnish. The moment we shook hands, I felt that if I hadn't already decided to kill her, she could have done with me whatever she wanted.

Her name is Lise. She doesn't say a great deal, like me. We understand each other without needing to speak, I think. And there's another thing I liked about her: after inspecting the surroundings – very superficially, I have to say – she stopped open-mouthed in front of the crayfish I stuffed last week. She took a careful hold of the little creature and placed it in the palm of her left hand. She didn't take her eyes off it.

I wouldn't have thought I'd one day meet someone, more to the point a woman, who might stand open-mouthed in front of my work for such a long time. Not even Joël has ever done that. It was as if she was looking… I don't know. At something that was both fascinating and terrifying at the same time. A snake or a candle flame. Standing stock-still in her heels, she murmured, 'It's so red, so red.' (I painted the crayfish as if it were cooked.) At that moment, a dark shadow passed across her eyes. She put the animal back down on the sheet and uttered these scarcely believable words:

— Monsieur Lefayen, you are an artist.

It won't be easy to kill her.

29 November

I didn't need to ask Lise to stay at the lighthouse. She invited herself for two nights. She phoned the sub-division and asked them to let her husband know. She obviously thought it necessary to say to me:

— They know how things are at my place.

I didn't ask questions. I never ask questions, be-cause I don't like it when people ask me questions. All I said was we would cause tongues to wag. I don't know why I said that. It was stupid. I felt stupid for saying it. But she smiled as she lit her cigarette.

Around one o'clock she wanted to be out in the sunshine. It was a nice day. I found her a spot that was sheltered from the wind and we spent our first afternoon together, just the two of us.

The two of us. How good it feels to write those words.

I've never really known the joy of holidays. The

sea, for me, is work. And when I'm on dry land, what else is there to do other than wait to get off it? I understand now the whole point of holidays for most people. For the first time in my life, I feel my body wanting to rest. I feel the exact opposite of what I normally feel when I embark on a holiday. Staring into space, my senses and muscles relaxing, I could almost have fallen asleep. I remained squatting at her feet, sensing once again, deep down, the doggie side of me.

As she slept with one arm behind her head, I approached and sniffed her armpit through her nylon blouse, taking care not to wake her. It smelt strong, it smelt good. I examined her legs, which were unevenly shaved, under flesh-coloured tights. My penis became hard as bone. I wanted to rub it against the hairy patches on her legs, or against her feet where they had been marked by the heels she had removed. Or simply just to show it to her, there, outside, in the sunshine. So I took it out and held it close to her mouth, which then I could no longer see. My heart was knocking in my chest. I started trembling all over. How I would have loved it if she had been pretending! But she wasn't pretending. She was sleeping peacefully, her mouth half-open, before my stiff prick. I stayed like that for two or three long minutes and I could no longer say what I was looking at, my prick or Lise's sleeping face.

I could have, sure, I could have. At least I could have masturbated. But I didn't. I find it easier to kill.

30 November

Yesterday we spent our first evening together. I cooked crayfish. She drank a lot, but didn't lose control.

Towards midnight, I showed her to the engineer's room. I had already removed my materials from the room and sprayed the walls with essence of lavender. We said goodnight.

That night was unlike most others, in that I slept long, a good seven hours, an achievement in itself, without dreams or nightmares. It was like the night gave me a break. This morning, I prepared a pot of coffee for Lise, which I brought to her room like a valet in a grand hotel, knocking softly on her door.

She was in bed in a short nightdress. I caught sight of her armpits, which were unshaven, and her breasts, which were heavy with large nipples. I'm sure she did it deliberately, showing herself off. I don't know how I restrained myself.

She asked me to stay while she drank her coffee. I sat down in the squat little armchair and waited.

She drank slowly, with little gulps. She seemed unaffected by how much she'd put away the night before.

Then, briskly, she pushed back the sheet to get up and I saw her cunt, fiery red and frizzy, like burning lichen, and it burned my eyes and my reason. I was unable to stop myself leaping on her like a seagull on an abandoned egg and planting my fingers either side of her pelvis, so I could make her wiggle it right in front of my mouth, and then on my mouth. The night smell made me insane with desire. While she struggled, I wiped my tongue over her like a flannel, until she gave me a smart slap on the forehead which made me stop and look up. She looked at me without smiling. It was a look that burned like ice. The corners of her mouth were turned down, her nose looked hard. I got the message right there and then and ran out of the room like a schoolboy caught in the girls' dorm.

A little later she found me in the kitchen. She acted like everything was normal. I had my nose in my coffee bowl with the chipped rim. She smiled at me. I blew on my coffee.

— Are we going fishing?

She made it sound like we were on holiday. I launched the *Poussée d'Archimède* and we put some lines out. I caught a three-and-a-quarter-pound bass.

During the whole afternoon I didn't dare look her in the eye. Or at any other part of her, for that matter, not even out of the corner of my eye.

Right now she's taking a shower. I think I can hear her singing.

We were on the boat when she said to me, somewhat wistfully, that she would like to stay longer than forty-eight hours. Me too, I'd also like her to stay longer than forty-eight hours. She can stay as long as she wants. She can stay for ever. In a moment I'll go and plant a stake facing the Gros Terrien sandbank, a stake for the dark night to come. If that cockroach Damien Lacassanne is messing about with his telescope, he won't see much because it won't be light like last time. Towards eleven o'clock, I'll call the subdivision to tell them that Lise was drunk, that she had a seizure or something like that, that she had wanted to go outside, and that I've been waiting for a while for her to come back. My voice will sound anxious. They'll alert the police and the police will turn up. If they decide to go over the place with a fine-tooth comb, they won't find a thing, not even the English couple, because, with the aid of an oar, I will have wrapped them all around the first marker buoy at Chevrier bank.

I'll go back and pick them up when the cops have left. I'll slip on the Egyptian jackal mask in honour of the beautiful Lise and I won't be answerable for what I'll do with her before relieving her of her entrails.

2 December

When Lise accompanied me yesterday evening as far as the point, it was about eight o'clock. She was filthy drunk, even more so than the night before. But I liked how she was when drunk, quiet and brooding in a way that suggested she might go a lot further.

She was carrying the bottle of hooch I use for scrubbing pans.

— That stake you planted this afternoon, you want to tie me to it at some point, right?

I shuddered. Lise threw her head back and laughed into the night.

— Sorry to bother you while you're working…

Then she gave a little 'hmm', either to conceal a burp or to express that particular lucidity that alcoholics can sometimes possess and that cannot quite be put into words.

I didn't react. We had arrived.

Lise grabbed the bag out of my hands, threw it in a heap at the foot of the stake and promptly sat on it.

I was distraught. My fists in my pockets reacted like my testicles in the cold. Perhaps, on this occasion, talking would help.

— Do… Do you ever think about death?

Lise's eyes didn't find mine straight away.

— Death?

She drank a mouthful of alcohol and stuck the half-empty bottle in the sand, top down.

— No.

Her head fell.

— And if you were to die, here and now, do you think you'd live again, up there?

Lise picked herself up and gave me a funny look. Then she looked up at the sky, which was as black as a tyre.

— Up there? Where up there?

A faint smile alighted on her lips. She took her lighter out of her pocket and went as if to set fire to the alcohol-soaked sand.

— To live again, first of all you need to have lived. Paradise should not be overpopulated.

She pulled the bottle out of the sand and wiped the neck with her finger.

— But if you had to die, right here, right now, how would you want to die?

She was getting tired but continued to reply to my annoying questions, as if obliged to do so.

— How would I like to die? Well, I'd like to die… at the bottom.

— At the bottom?

74

— At the bottom of the Indian Ocean. Surrounded by fish of all different colours.

I was reminded of the Cousteau documentary of the other day.

— That's beautiful, I said.

— Something I've never seen. I've just seen plenty of fucking wrecks. Wrecks like me. Zinc carcasses in Italy. Cargo ships off Sardinia. There's nothing stupider than a sunken wreck. Nothing so gnawed at. Nothing sadder.

Lise licked the neck of the bottle. There was still some sand on it, here and there in little patches. She asked a question.

— Have you ever been diving?

— No.

— Shame. If you don't kill me, I'll teach you. And in return you can teach me to stuff crayfish so they live for ever.

It was cold, but Lise lifted up her skirt. Spread her legs.

— Shine a light.

I took out my light and shone it. Pubic hair escaped from her knickers, on both sides. Her pelvis swayed gently, as if about to take flight. She was giving me permission.

I buried my head between her legs and used my teeth to pull her knickers to one side, then chewed on her cunt like it was gum. She panted and instructed me, 'Harder,' loud enough for me to hear over the sound of the ocean. Her fingers were digging into my scalp to the point where I imagined them breaking the skin and blood flowing.

It wasn't long before I had to get my cock out. My mouth wasn't enough for her.

— Shine a light on that.

I pointed the torch at it. Lise brushed it with her fingertips like a sign of respect.

— It's so beautiful. It's so big. I could hang off it and it wouldn't bend. What a wonderful way to go... To die hanging off your prick. Come to me.

I'm a big guy, sure, as I've said, but sticking it to a woman I'm not paying is a new experience for me. 'Fuck me, fuck me, fuck me,' she shouted as naturally as breathing. 'Faster, harder,' she demanded. 'Do it,' she said, and some longer exhortation rendered unintelligible by my thrusting loins. When she wasn't actually speaking, her tongue would be hanging half out of her mouth. I licked it. Under her armpits the blouse she'd been wearing the day before was no match for my teeth. I buried my nose in a tuft of strong-smelling hair and moved my head vigorously in a circular motion, inhaling deeply through my nose all the while. I think the last time I fucked her she was out of it. Perhaps the last two times. But I didn't give a fuck, and, every time she came, a lion roared, the king of the animals at the foot of the king of the lighthouses, a lion with a mane the colour of Lise's hair, an enormous lion, a man-eater that refuses to end up a set of bagpipes.

The waves washed at the base of the stake. I picked Lise up in my arms. I carried her, like the man had carried her ashore three days before, and like a young groom carries his bride across the threshold of the family home.

She weighed nothing.

While walking with her in my arms I didn't take my eyes off hers. Her face was marked by a deep line between her eyebrows.

I stopped for breath. Where we were, Joël's son would have been able to see us, but who cares, I wasn't doing anything wrong.

Lise woke up. She smiled faintly and said:

— You're kind.

Kind, yes… Finally someone sees it! Suddenly I was walking on air and I ran and ran and ran and threw Lise up in front of me like a teddy bear and I laughed and laughed and laughed because I was so happy and I cried as well for the same reason, because, suddenly, I no longer wanted to kill anyone.

Lise didn't want me to stay in her bed. So I curled up in the little armchair and thought again about the English couple.

They brought love here. Me and Lise, that's thanks to them. When they're done, which will be soon, before I weigh them down and throw them in the sea, I will give them a beautiful ceremony. I might even discuss it with Lise.

3 December

This morning I was with Lise on the beach. She was carrying her boots in a plastic bag.

Once the dinghy was in view she whispered into my ear:

— It'll be me you speak to now on the radio. We'll have to act professional. You understand, Geoffroy. Professional.

— Yes.

She leaned in again, closer this time.

— As for the English couple, my lips are sealed. The cops came by the subdivision. You've got nothing to worry about. They'll be looking for their bodies as far as Talmont. Drowned, they reckon.

She shouted to the guy on the bridge:

— Come a bit closer.

Lise got me to clasp my hands around her lighter. She repeated:

— My lips are sealed.

— What might you otherwise say, Lise? What could there be to say?

She didn't reply. The guy arrived. She lifted her arms in readiness, her cigarette between her lips.

I remained rooted to the spot, dazed, filled with love, fear and self-disgust, all at the same time. Especially self-disgust.

From the bridge of the dinghy Lise shouted:

— Next month, will you teach me how to prepare crayfish, for ever and ever?

I headed back inside without delay, feeling agitated. Lise must have discovered the bodies in the cellar, perhaps the night I'd slept well. Either that or she'd found my diary.

More and more she has a hold over me.

To take my mind off things I went up to the lantern gallery with a bucket of catfish and crushed velvet crabs. I tried going *kee-ya* and *kree-aaa*, then *kyow, kyow, kyow*. Finally a herring gull heard me, then ten, then twenty. Once the bucket was empty, the birds hung around for a bit then flew off amid a chorus of raucous cries.

I was alone again. I didn't feel good. I walked down the steps to the bottom, then walked back up, then walked down again and walked back up and ended up collapsing on the gallery.

I wrapped myself in one of the canvas covers, thinking it would be good to be a corpse.

I held my breath for as long as I could.

Why was I not born looking on the bright side?

Why do I have this lump of coal as big as a lemon in my stomach that stains my fingers when I touch it? Why has it spread to my brain?

I don't want to join my mother in the nuthouse. The last time I saw her, eight years ago, she got out a crucifix, shoved it under my nose and demanded I kiss it.

— Say sorry to your father! Say sorry!

— Sorry for what, Mother?

— Sorry for your brother, who laid the table for you. You must atone. You must atone!

It's absolutely necessary that I resuscitate the English couple as soon as possible. It's absolutely necessary that I atone. If not, they'll lock me up, whether it's in prison or in the nuthouse, and I'll never see Lise again as long as I live. I survived my father. I survived my mother. I survived Monsieur Rouleau. I survived the two Rogers. But as for being locked up, I wouldn't survive that.

4 December

How has Lise changed my life? Well, she could throw a stick in twenty-foot-high waves and I wouldn't hesitate for a moment. The lighthouse is no longer my master. I'm even wondering what it is I'm doing here and I'm not sure I want to stay any longer. The beauty of Cordouan, with its royal embellishments, has faded in Lise's shadow. That's how she has changed my life: she has killed the lighthouse.

I had a dog once, a long time ago, mongrel, part cocker spaniel, who one day fell under the wheels of a dangerous driver. The dog escaped with some hair loss and a displaced pelvis. However, he was in so much pain he wouldn't let me touch him. He'd have bitten me. I took him to a bonesetter who made him yelp and afterwards it was all over. My dog was fixed. I can still see the look in his eyes, in the moment the procedure was over. He looked around as if he'd just regained his sight. He jumped into the arms of the bonesetter and licked and licked and licked him, wagging his tail with great enthusiasm and making a whining noise like he hadn't made since he was a puppy. My dog adored me, but he never showed me as much love as he showed the bonesetter that day.

Lise fixes me like the bonesetter fixed my dog. Better still, she arms me, she gives me armour-plating, like a crayfish. When the cops phoned, I wasn't afraid.

— I'm not saying we spend our whole lives looking through it, but there's no denying, with the telescope, it's like you're right there.

That little devil Damien Lacassanne had given them the idea.

— From the beach at Verdon, Monsieur Lefayen, you can see the rock at Gros Terrien.

— You've got no right to watch me.

He couldn't possibly have seen me with Lise the other evening, because of the weather. However:

— Why so determined with the stake the morning before the engineer's departure, Monsieur Lefayen?

The tide had prevented me from acting before sunrise. So they'd been able to see me freeing the stake.

— It's not against the law to plant a stake in the beach. I wanted a mooring post to fish from. Then I changed my mind.

— You're right, it's not a good idea. Surprising, a sea salt coming up with an idea like that.

— I buried it two metres in the sand, so it would hold.

— You're right, it's none of our business. You can plant and dig up all the stakes you want, Monsieur

Lefayen. You can even go rowing around the rocks with an engineer from Lighthouses and Beacons who happens to be of the female gender.

He'd definitely seen us then.

— She wanted to go fishing.

— Monsieur Lefayen, I'm not winding you up. Consider it a friendly warning: Lise Tricoul is in and out of mental hospital.

— Doesn't mean she's crazy.

— It does when she's sectioned.

— Why are you telling me this?

— The subdivision asked us to warn you.

— Why doesn't she tell me herself?

— Medical confidentiality.

— If she was as mad as you say, they wouldn't let her work unsupervised. She behaved perfectly normally.

— I don't doubt it, Monsieur Lefayen. I don't doubt it.

He went on a bit more about Lise: she was an alcoholic, which I knew, and a pathological liar. Last year she nearly killed her husband and daughter, who Lise accused – wrongly, it seemed, after an investigation – of sleeping with her father.

I didn't know how seriously to take what they were telling me.

They didn't mention the English couple. I didn't know if that was a good sign or a bad sign.

Why didn't they come over? It's pretty straightforward from Verdon. Why let me know they're watching me? Because they don't think I've done anything wrong? In which case, why watch me?

Or could it be Lise they wanted to keep an eye on?

Maybe they saw me with her in the afternoon on the ring showing my dick to the seagulls.

Maybe they questioned the guys who came on the first supply vessel. If so, they'll know I shut myself away in the watch room, that I asked for salt and that there was a bad smell in the cellar.

Why did they go to Joël's place?

I don't like cops. I've always been worried about mistakes, an error that would send me to prison instead of someone else.

9 December

I haven't done much this week apart from daydreaming. And that gave me a great idea, but one that would demand a lot of courage. Every day I scrape together a little bit more from the bottom of my soul. I need more and more, a ton of it.

The weather has been really bad lately. The wind howling enough to make you go mad. At least it should discourage the telescope fans.

I've been devoting myself to the English couple, who I've moved to the House of Perfection, under the lantern. I've set them so they're sitting down, hand in hand. I'm filling out their lips and Katleen's chest, having closed the eye-sockets with balls of fabric. Soon I'll apply another coat of resin, but not before I've stained them with yellow ochre and red ochre. Then I'll glaze the faces, stitch the fingernails, then soak the hands and feet in a bath of henna. I'm already thinking about displays. I have a few simple but hopefully effective ideas inspired by the fauna and flora of the rocks and rock pools.

Otherwise I'm watching lots of TV. A report on narwhals, another on deep-sea fish, which for some reason made me think of Lise, and then a third on a stunning fight between a cobra and a mongoose. For the first time in my life, I reckon, I felt sympathy for a snake. It was erect on its coils, leaning back slightly, immobile as a lighthouse, its head swelling like the chest of a cocksure adolescent. It looked the mongoose up and down, while the mongoose tried to distract it by forever hopping from one of its back feet to the other like a boxer with ringworm, its tail up and mouth open. Sometimes the mongoose dropped down on all fours and arched its back with its hair standing on end. It thwarted all of the cobra's attacks and returned to its crazy dance routine. It owned that snake in the end.

The disgust I felt for the mongoose was greater than my fear of the snake. I imagined this great long-haired rat curled up in a ball in a corner somewhere pulling apart the remains of the snake like a string of liquorice. I saw its mean little eyes looking all worried as it digested its trophy and waited for hunger to strike again. Then it would skulk off on its next hunt and so the pitiless cycle began again. I had to get up to go and be sick.

14 December

This morning I said to myself, 'It has to be today.'

I know, it's unwise, with the police. Discovering I'm madly in love with a madwoman, as they call her, could easily make them doubly suspicious. But too bad.

When I call the subdivision every day, it's not Lise I speak to and it's not Lise who responds. It's the engineer from Lighthouses and Beacons I speak to and the engineer from Lighthouses and Beacons who responds. And it's not me who speaks but the lighthouse keeper in a voice no more familiar than the cop the other day. Professional, as Lise said.

But today, the man Geoffroy Lefayen, whose heart resembles a hedgehog curled up in a ball, wondered how he might be able to walk in the footsteps of lighthouse keeper Geoffroy Lefayen. So the man Geoffroy Lefayen thought about the cunt and armpits of the woman Lise Tricoul to give himself courage.

I said to her on the radio:

— Call me on the phone. Right now.

Waiting for the phone to ring, I thought I was about to get myself told off. But no.

— Is that you?

— Yes.

— How are you?

— Fine. Well, not really. I miss you.

— That's normal. You're all alone.

— I don't miss anyone else. Only you.

— I'll be back. You just need to hang on.

— You're coming back?

— I said so, didn't I?

— We'll do again what we did.

— Even better.

She seemed clear on that.

— Lise.

— Yes?

— I need to talk to you about something.

Not about death, I hope. I don't like it when you talk about death. I don't like it when you talk at all, in fact.

She lowered her voice.

— I prefer it when you fuck me.

Her words had an immediate effect, but I had enough self-control not to lose my train of thought.

— Well. I...

A seagull's nest had become lodged in my throat.

— I want you to be my wife.

Neither of us spoke for a moment.

— Your wife?

I swallowed saliva.

— Yes.

Lise sounded agitated.

— I'm just going to shut the door.

I heard her heels giving the floor over there a good hammering and the images that came into my mind made my cock expand like the head of that cobra the other day on the TV.

— Your wife… Perhaps you weren't aware that I'm married.

— I know, but that's not a problem. You can get divorced. Seems your husband…

I heard a loud report as heel met floor, like a slap. Then an outburst:

— What do you know about my husband?

— Nothing. That it's not that great between the two of you, that's all.

— That's no reason to marry the first guy who comes along.

I could feel my heart thumping, and my voice was no longer my own.

— I'm not the first guy who comes along. I love you.

It just popped out, like a worm. Lise calmed down a little.

— If women had to marry every man they slept with there'd be a queue outside the register office.

— Is that a no, then?

— You don't get married because of one good shag.

— I'm not asking you to give me an answer right now.

— Right now or in a hundred years the answer is

still no. Being on your own is messing with your head.

Lise was speaking but I'd stopped listening. I slammed the phone down with such force the receiver broke apart. The phone rang again immediately, but I didn't answer it. I saw white before my eyes, as if I was in the middle of a desert. And then the walls started advancing towards me and I was forced to defend myself. My Adam's apple pressed up against the stone. I dug my nails into Cordouan. 'Fucking lighthouse,' I yelled, at a deafening volume, a thousand times. I ran up and down the stairs faster even than the other day, to stem the flow of tears. I went out on to the gallery. It was pouring with rain. I stayed there maybe an hour in the hope it would cleanse my soul. I closed my eyes and put my fist through a window. The sight of blood calmed me a little, but not enough to stop me putting my other fist through another window. I daubed my face with my own blood, which the rain soon caused to run, in rivulets, down my shirt. I've no idea why, but I thought of my father and my brother Geoffroy, and fresh tears mixed with the rain and my blood.

The English couple have been amazing. When I sat myself down between them, they didn't make the slightest move to repel the friendly jackal who's going to lead them, out of the kindness of his heart, to paradise. They're my friends, the English couple. Real friends who don't betray you.

15 December

Six in the morning and I'm picking up from yesterday after a severe headache forced me to put down my pen last night.

So, yesterday evening, I was downstairs when the phone rang around eight o'clock. I had already replaced the glass in the lantern, washed away the blood and bandaged my hands. Maybe it would be Lise…

— Geoffroy?

It was Joël.

— How's it going?

— I feel lousy.

— Nothing serious?

— Nothing serious.

— Anyway, I didn't tell you the other day, the cops came to the house, in connection with an English couple who've gone missing, which I imagine you know about.

— Why did they come to you?

— The Englishman phoned me two months ago. He was interested in the lighthouse. I suggested he drop by and we had a chat over a drink. It was my wife who let the police know. She was concerned they'd find out and think it was odd we hadn't mentioned it.

Joël sounded worried. He continued.

— Anyway. I didn't tell the police about Damien having seen three people on the beach the other day. But it's possible Damien told them himself.

— Yes, he did.

— He promised not to say anything to his mother.

— Good. She'd make something of it.

— I hope it won't cause you any trouble.

— What kind of trouble?

— You never know with the police. Especially the one who came here. He had one of those faces. So you're not cross with Damien?

— I'm not cross with Damien.

— There was no malice. You know Damien. He was nervous, that's all.

— It's fine. Really.

— I was calling also to let you know about the next supply trip, which will be next week. I'll be taking care of it myself. Well, that's if I feel better. There's going to be strong winds until Christmas apparently. If it's at all possible I'll come with Damien. Is there anything you want me to bring?

— …

— Geoffroy?

— …

— Well, answer, you so-and-so.

— Don't come, Joël. Don't come.

— Something wrong, Geoffroy?

— Don't come. Neither on your own, nor with Damien.

21 December

I've been in bed for four days. Company has consist-
ed of my stuffed crayfish, my one-eyed teddy bear
and the juvenile gull with a damaged wing that I
found on the gallery the day before yesterday. There's
something poignant about a juvenile gull with its
plumage flecked with an undefinable shade of grey
and its slightly superior air. A gust of wind must have
dashed it against the lantern, unless it was attracted
by the light. That can happen. To start with, he tried
to peck me, but then relaxed. I dried him off, fed him
with mussels and old bits of cheese, and I improvised
a splint out of balsa wood. He doesn't seem to mind
being attached to a stone by a length of sisal and has
already improved.

I, on the other hand, must have a touch of fever.
I'm afraid of everything, even of the English couple
during the night. It's not good.

Good God, but I'm cold! I must have caught my death in the rain last Monday. I've got no appetite. Which is just as well as the fridge is empty.

I don't feel like going fishing and anyway the sea is too rough these days. I've reduced radio use to once a day. TV bores me. Even writing is a slog as I hurt everywhere, in my back, my eyes, my hands.

When Joël arrived I was asleep in the engineer's room with the door locked. I'd also blocked the postern.

I heard Joël's voice.

— Open up, Geoffroy. It's us.

— Go away.

I must have surprised them, as they didn't reply straight away.

— Don't be stubborn. We've got a doctor with us. You didn't seem right on Thursday.

Joël had phoned on Thursday. Apologising again. Stupidly I'd let on about the fever.

— He can go to hell. I don't need anyone.

— You're in a bad way, Geoffroy. He'll sort you out.

— I've told you, I'm fine. I don't want to see anyone.

— Geoffroy, listen. We'll go and stretch our legs. Be back in a bit. If you haven't opened up, we'll come up the ladder.

That gave me enough time to take a chisel to the top six rungs of the ladder. After which I hid in the engineer's room again.

They came back.

— For God's sake, Geoffroy, have you gone completely mad?

— Like I said, go away.

They didn't reply.

— Fuck off!

— Not till we've seen you.

— You're not seeing me. You won't see me again.

I decided to keep quiet and wait for the tide to take them away. I heard an unknown voice.

— Monsieur Lefayen?

It was the doctor. I let the wind reply on my behalf.

— Let me see you.

The wind again.

— I have to examine you. There'll be something you can take from the medicine cupboard. Just let me…

I gathered my strength and yelled above the wind:

— Fuck off! Fuck off, all of you!

Five whole minutes went by, maybe ten, before they realised they were wasting their time.

— All right, Geoffroy, we're off. Damien has tied a bag of supplics to the ladder. There's some medicine there as well. We'll be back, Geoffroy.

The sound of a motor told me they had been telling the truth. I got up and jumped out on to the roof of the ring. Joël waved to me from the boat and shouted but his words were swallowed by the wind. I walked to the ladder and untied a large canvas sack like an army kitbag. The bottom of it was only inches from the ocean.

It contained several slightly overdone loaves of bread, some second-rate fruit and veg, a large pot of honey, cheese and milk, numerous jars of jam, a bottle of decent cognac and a bottle of Pineau, a nice mallard to pluck, a block of foie gras, a little Christmas tree and some plastic baubles, an ugly crib with what you'd expect, a cow, a donkey, three wise men and baby Jesus, a shop-bought buttercream Christmas cake and four boxes of Vybramicine 500.

I kept the duck and the drink and chucked the rest of the crap in the sea.

22 December

Joël called yesterday, as soon as he was back on dry land.

— You're in a bad way, mate.

— What's the weather like in Royan?

— What do you think? The same as where you are, in your bloody lighthouse, of course. It's getting to you. It's been almost three months. They'll have to replace you. I'll have a word.

— I'll be fine.

— Why wouldn't you see me, Geoffroy? Because of Damien and the police, is that it?

— Nothing to do with Damien and the police.

— What, then?

— You wouldn't understand, Joël. You wouldn't understand.

25 December

Feeling a bit better. Christmas Eve was nice, spent in the company of Katleen and Steeven and three of my most beautiful crayfish. I didn't eat. It was all about friendship, which is the most important thing.

On the other hand, I knocked back the bottle of cognac, downed it in one, more or less. After that, things got a bit vague. I hope I wasn't too familiar with Katleen.

I woke up this morning with a hangover. It's the first time in my career I've forgotten to switch off the light. Forgetting to switch it on would have been worse, but still, it's not great. The lighthouse keeper from La Coubre called me three times, but I only heard him on the third attempt. Same goes for Joël, who had checked in with the guy at La Coubre. He also went on about my health and I tried to reassure him once and for all, so that he'd give it a rest. Again he talked about calling the subdivision.

— Do that and I'll kill you.

It just came out, like when I said 'I love you' to Lise the other day. It must have sounded like I meant it.

— Well, that's nice. I'm only trying to help you.

— You're obsessed with the lighthouse, Joël. Forget about the lighthouse. It's not good for you.

— You're the one who's obsessed with the lighthouse, Geoffroy. Classic symptoms: when you think you're all right, you're not. It's like you've got no idea. Like you've never done this job before.

— I'm not going to take advice from someone who got caught out looking at the lantern. You know what, Joël? Piss off. Just piss off.

Next I sat around stupidly waiting for a call from the real Lise, not radio Lise. That's all I did: wait, sitting on the floor with my back against the wall, as if it was an important activity that required everything of a man, every fibre of his being.

Outside, the weather ate up the minutes and the hours. My fifty-second Christmas is all about waiting for Lise.

This evening I managed to find a little bit of energy. I got stuck into Joël's mallard. I'm operating in the kitchen this time. I placed it on a clean piece of cardboard and made an incision from the rump to the head, taking care not to cut any feathers. I separated the skin from the body. Cut the bones in the wings and feet and severed the neck. Pulled the skin from the skull, taking great care around the eyes, and removed the tongue. I turned the creature over carefully and… my head dropped. My hands had let me down. I'd pierced the glands that contain the duck's waterproofing oils and this stained the feathers.

That's the first time that's happened to me.

If I can no longer give life to the dead, I'm only good for the scrapheap.

I'm starting to wonder if this lighthouse might be cursed. A short while ago I laid into the walls of the chapel with a knife. It felt like I was attacking a sibling. 'Serves you right,' I repeated over and over, even though I knew it was pointless. Then I went outside, in spite of the dark and the rain that was falling so hard it felt like hail. I whacked the sledgehammer as hard as I could against the huge concrete slabs that cover the slimy stone at the base of the lighthouse.

The monster remained deaf and immobile. But maybe within, deep inside the entrails, they could hear me – my father, my mother, my brother, Monsieur Rouleau and the two Rogers.

27 December

It's true that lately I've been more tired than usual, physically and mentally, but, apart from Christmas Day, I've stuck at it, the radio and everything, and I always fill in the log, and I know that this machine inside me will never break down, whatever happens, like the lighthouse is one of my vital organs, or my small child, or my old man who can't quite feed himself.

What I don't know, on the other hand, is when I'm my normal self. Am I in some kind of a trance when I'm concentrating on the lighthouse, and myself the rest of the time, or the other way around? For example, I can't explain why I was out on the rocks getting myself all worked up yesterday. Perhaps I needed exercise. Or it's all Lise's fault. Yes, Lise is driving me round the bend. But it's no reason to destroy everything, or go on hunger strike, as I have been these last few days.

I'm not the type of person to mope for long: this morning, after a couple of goes at Joël's mallard, I took advantage of a lull to put the *Poussée d'Archimède* in the water, just to see if I was still capable of catching anything. I was daydreaming, about Lise no doubt, my rod between my knees, bent double but freshly shaved, when the boat struck a fifty-litre barrel exactly like the one that had sat on two breeze blocks in Old Man Rouleau's cellar (the old bastard made me go and fetch his plonk every evening when he knew I was scared stiff of the toads that lived in the basement). It was full. Back at the lighthouse I made a hole in it with a corkscrew and in no time had taken a mouthful of genuine old timer's hooch. It tasted of nuts, or of figs, but either way it was definitely original. That was the next two hours accounted for: I set about decanting it into the fifty half-bottles and twenty old litre bottles stored in one of the cellars. To my great surprise, the barrel was empty before I'd filled even half of the bottles. I shook it. It was still heavy. I shook it harder and felt something give and knock, a muffled sound, slightly sad somehow. I undid a cap and found within an adorable little monkey dripping in brandy, curled up in the foetal position, magnificently well preserved.

I was so happy I took her in my arms before I'd even rubbed her down. Too bad about my jacket, which would now stink of alcohol. I threw her up in the air to celebrate, just as I had with Lise the other day out on the rocks. Immediately I took her to introduce her to my little family. Baby conger, lovely crayfish and nice mallard not yet finished, pretty seagull convalescing, and of course my friends Katleen and Steeven.

I made a place for Sheeta in my bedroom next to my one-eyed bear. I felt calmer than I had in a long time.

28 December

Today has been pretty much like yesterday, which is to say reasonably peaceful.

Lise should really not have called just now, as she caused all of that to change. Suddenly, I don't know what kind of night I'm going to have, or rather I know only too well.

— We can replace you if you like. There is someone.

— Let him try.

Lise was dead drunk. She was searching for her words.

— I'm not coming after all.

— Because of me.

— Because of the pope.

— Who'll come, then?

— I don't care. Maybe a woman. Who knows? You can fuck her as well.

— Don't talk like that.

— You can get your cock out for her while she's asleep. That's what I liked.

So she'd seen me the other day, acting like an idiot. If the cops were listening in…

— Why can't you come?

— I've got a lot on.

— Work?

— No, my bastard of a husband.

— What about your bastard of a husband?

— His stomach is too hairy. He's got his mother's legs. He stinks and calls me names. He treats me like I'm his mother and fucks my daughter and that bitch believes every word he says. On top of which, he doesn't like scuba diving.

— I like scuba diving.

— I'm going to kill him, Geoffroy.

— Don't say that.

— Him and his great big hairy belly, his old lady legs and his foul breath.

— I don't want you getting into trouble.

— I won't get into trouble. I'm clever. Just as clever as you. I'll go over there, after.

— Over where?

— The madhouse. I'm fine there. I'm crazy when I'm there, but I'm fine. I'm better around mad people than normal people.

— You're not crazy, Lise.

— My doctor tells me that as well. It doesn't stop him conniving with my husband to get me locked up.

— Come to the lighthouse.

— I'm not coming. Even if I've never met a kinder idiot than you.

I know you won't come. And I know that you're capable of killing your husband.

I also know that I must resign myself to years of solitude.

Tonight, the wind will howl in my skull like death.

I need friends, real flesh-and-blood friends. I've had enough of soft toys and mummies. I need friends, I need a dog. If I had one wish it would be that someone send me a dog.

1 January

The first people to wish me a Happy New Year were the police. They called around eight in the morning. They had news concerning the search for the English couple, they said. But they didn't say what and I didn't ask.

It wasn't like the other times. I liked the sound of this one's voice.

He didn't interrogate me and he didn't talk about Lise.

At the beginning there were plenty of gaps in the conversation. He must have been doing it on purpose to unsettle me.

Then he fired off a load of random questions. How long had I been interested in taxidermy (Joël must have been blabbing again), what kind of soldier had I been, did I have brothers and sisters, et cetera? Did I this, did I that...? I don't really see what it's got to do with him whether I got on with my parents when I was a kid.

He must be good, this guy, because he got me to feel I could trust him. I revealed intimate family details that I would normally be too ashamed to talk about. I even confessed to a few things in connection with Old Man Rouleau, and not only the most harmless.

He listened without interrupting. Never in my life had I confided in someone to that extent. I hope I didn't give too much away.

I repeat, this guy is very good.

In a gentle voice, he said to me, 'I'll come and see you soon, Monsieur Lefayen,' adding: 'My name is Jacques.'

When he hung up I realised I was looking forward to speaking to him again.

Jacques is a friend. He did me as much good as Lise did the other day. More, even.

4 January

There is a god of lighthouse keepers. I have a dog, a purebred red setter. He's called Bambi. He has red hair like Lise, perhaps the reason he reminds me of her so much. He must be scarcely one year old. He's always out of breath. I like that in a dog. At low tide I let him out on the beach and he chases seagulls. He's bound to end up catching one, he's so lively. He comes back covered in wet sand and seaweed and it gives me pleasure to dry him off. 'Good dog, good dog,' I say. He responds by barking. On the other hand, at midday I had to tell him off, as he almost polished off my lame seagull, which I had left on the sideboard in the kitchen. He no doubt wanted to let me know it was lunchtime. I removed the skin from a boiled mullet, which he finally ate after initially turning up his nose. I know you're not a cat, Bambi, but there's only fish to be had around here. You'd better get used to it.

The whole of Royan, the whole of Le Verdon and all the amateur sailors from roundabout must know that you're here, since I never stop you going out and running around. You're a gundog. It's what you do. If anyone asks me where you came from, I'll say, with a shrug and a lift of my eyebrows and a little farty noise from my lips: 'Well, he arrived one morning, by boat, I expect.' And I'll chuck a stick for you, to show that I'm bored of stupid questions.

When I heard barking on the beach, I thought it was the wind, which was strong that evening. But I also heard voices and a knock on the door.

I only had eyes for you. Your masters looked like three complete idiots. Three Spaniards or three Portuguese, I don't know. Can you tell me, little Bambi, why they thought it would be a good idea to hold a gun to my head, as if the lighthouse was a bank and I was a teller? If they'd turned up all sweetness and light saying they had engine trouble and could they possibly spend the night in the lighthouse and fix it in the morning, I'd have said, 'Yes, of course…'

Yeah. You're right. I'd have killed them anyway.

5 January

I know now that they were on the run. The coast-guard called me this evening to let me know about a 'suspect' Spanish boat, as they put it.

They were hungry. Bad luck, the fridge has been empty for ages. One of them must have thought I was winding them up and gave me a slap. He caught me with his great big watch. They rooted through the cupboards and then talked among themselves. I didn't understand a word, but sensed the urgency from the tone of their voices and the look in their eyes.

The guy who had hit me returned to their boat, possibly to look for something to eat.

They should have chosen to go without for a night. You'll say, even against three, I'd have had a go. Even against ten.

The nasty little prick who'd kept his gun stuck against

my temple received a whack to his own temple from my crayfish pan, with such force I thought I might have killed him outright. You remember the other guy, Bambi, the one with his arse sticking out and his body in a kind of half-crouch with a flick knife in his hand? Like I'd be frightened of him. I grabbed my general-purpose cleaver, which I use whether I'm removing fish scales or heads or finely chopping parsley, and approached him quite calmly. You were wagging your tail. His knife went flying and I flattened his hand on the table. Four entire phalanges and three half-phalanges joined his knife flying through the air. I had to knock him out he was making so much noise.

I went outside before I had time to cool down. The third guy knew how to fight. He caught me twice, once in the eye, once on the jaw. He was stocky and his punches carried weight. I don't know much about fighting, but it's as well not to let me make contact, because I never need to land a punch twice. I came down with all my force on his neck. He grimaced and fell to his knees. He was fucked.

I grabbed him around the wrist, the wrist his great big watch was on, and dragged him to the foreshore. It's odd, but it was at that moment I felt my full strength.

The guy's head banged on a few rocks. I sat him down in a pool, but he collapsed again. Using my hands I ladled mud on to his face and meticulously coated him – his face, his neck and collarbone, even his forearms.

I gave him a good old mud shampoo.

Then I rubbed seaweed on him so he'd smell of the sea.

Blood trickled slowly out of his nose. He was dying, or he'd just died, or he was about to die. Details. I was absorbed by the sight of his blood, which formed a narrow ribbon from his nostril to the bleeding veins in his neck. I had a sudden desire to use it like vermilion, to daub a giant canvas with it and sign it with a handprint, like the first humans on the walls of caves.

I think I stayed like that for some time, fantasising I was an artist.

The cold brought me back to the lighthouse. I dragged my bundle after me as before and threw him down on the steps in front of the postern because he had started to weigh me down.

Catching sight of me, you celebrated. How big you were, up on your hind legs. 'Good dog, good dog,' I said. You licked the blood off my hands and wanted to play, but it wasn't the right time. I had to deal with the two jerks who were still cluttering up my kitchen.

I tied them up and hauled them up to the gallery. Like their colleague's on the rocks outside, their heads banged on the steps, two hundred and ninety times.

You followed us, barking. I could read the plea in your eyes: 'Play, play.' I said, 'Yes, soon. Daddy's nearly finished.'

Up on the gallery, I placed my sacks of meat against the green window, which made them look even worse. I'm sorry, Bambi, for closing the door on you, but I feared the lamp might burn your hazel eyes, your beautiful hazel eyes, like it burned Joël's.

And then I didn't want you to see your daddy tying the men up by their feet, knotting the rope on the railing and dangling them over the side head first. That's not a nice sight for a dog.

Especially when one of them came to and started moaning about 'pity'.

— Pity? I said. What for? You should be thanking me for allowing you to die hanging off a great big cock. I knew someone whose dream it was to die like that.

When I dragged them back up, the one who'd had his hand cut off was still alive. For a moment I pictured myself caring for him. Washing him, warming him up, going fishing for him, cooking for him, feeding him, monitoring his progress day by day, as I monitor that of my young seagull. But I thought Bambi might be jealous. The seagull was quite enough. And then the guy would probably just be ungrateful once he'd perked up. So I finished him off.

When I opened the door, there you were, Bambi, celebrating again. You were so excited you nearly sent me tumbling down the stairs with my two packages on my shoulders. 'Play, play,' said your eyes. 'Good dog, good dog,' said mine.

Those losers didn't even deserve salt up their arses and an improvised cork from whatever was to hand. I loaded them on to the *Poussée d'Archimède*, which I dragged down to the waterline. I took it out as far as their boat, to which I tied mine. I hauled the bodies up on to the bridge and lashed them to the anchor, once I'd raised it.

While I was busy doing this, the boat had drifted,

as I'd hoped it would. I had a nose around in the cabin but the fridge and the cupboards on the boat were as impoverished as those in the lighthouse. Nevertheless I found four cans of food that I wolfed down cold, with my fingers, without ever really knowing what I was eating, because all that carry-on had given me an enormous appetite. There was also a six-pack that I knocked back in no time.

I went out on to the bridge. We were quite far away. I went back down and, using the sledgehammer and the iron bar that I'd brought with me, made two holes in the hull. Then without dawdling I jumped into the flat-bottomed boat and started rowing in the direction of the lighthouse.

Their boat sank in five minutes.

It took me a good half-hour to get back to the beach, a wind having got up. You were waiting for me, tail wagging. We'd known each other barely two hours. Finally we'd get to play.

January

Was I seen from the coast the other evening? I don't give a fuck. Something bad has happened. My seagull is dead.

I found it dangling from the cornice of the sideboard, like a game bird hanging from a hook in the butcher's.

Bambi looked at it sadly. I swear, that dog's as sensitive as I am.

I took it down and caressed it. It was still warm. I'm a little embarrassed to admit it, but I cried. I recalled the young blackbird I saved when I was still at Old Man Rouleau's. I'd christened him Geoffroy, not for me but for my brother, and made him a little nest in a shoebox. I really liked his beak, which flattened out at the sides, making it look like he was pouting or sad. I opened my heart to Geoffroy. One evening, Rouleau found the shoebox. I had forgotten to hide it in my cupboard, which was what I'd do if I heard him coming. Geoffroy must have sensed that there was going to be trouble because he shrank back into one of the corners, a hunted look in his eye and with his head pulled right into his body. I can still hear the panicked sound of his feet against the cardboard, and then immediately afterwards the sound of his little bones when Rouleau suffocated him. 'A bird in the house is not hygienic. It could give you tuberculosis.' He chucked Geoffroy out of the window. I heard his body hit the ground, two floors below, and the silence immediately afterwards. Rouleau went to wash his filthy mitts, promising to give me a good hiding if I did it again. The following day I found Geoffroy. He was hard, cold and all tensed up, dead as a doornail. Cremating him was as much about not being able to bear the idea of him crawling with maggots as the trace of fingers that had soiled his little baby blackbird's body.

I'm not going to cremate my seagull and I'm not going to stuff him either. I'm going to give him to Bambi. That way he'll rejoin his own kind, in a way, when Bambi goes galloping after the seagulls on the beach. I blanched him and cooked him as if I was doing it for me. Seeing Bambi licking his chops alleviated some of my pain.

Rain

My seagull was a bad omen. This morning on the beach I found several dead black-headed gulls, herring gulls and even a cormorant. It's not news to anyone at the subdivision. The beaches are covered with them on the coast. There was a similar event ten years ago. They've never known what caused it. Researchers talked about the possibility of collective suicide.

I took the wheelbarrow down to the shore. The sun was shining. The tide deposited more corpses on the beach. Bambi didn't touch a single one, not even with his nose. Some of them weren't quite dead.

Within half an hour I had twenty birds in my wheelbarrow. I laid them out in a circle and lay down in the middle of it. My cheek touching the sand. I was dead and I was fine with that.

Evening

When Joël arrived with the supply vessel he found me in not too bad a state, if a little thin. We were on the beach.

— I'm glad you called. And I'm glad you asked us to bring you nice things. If you're feeling hungry, then you must be feeling better. I didn't forget the champagne. It's true I didn't bring any at Christmas. You know, that last time, I was worried about you. If I didn't call on New Year's Day it's because I told myself you'd think—

— It's all right, Joël.

We talked about the seagulls. On the coast, firemen have been deployed to collect them.

Damien had come with his dad. I said to the kid:

— Seen anything interesting lately through your telescope?

He went red.

— I… I don't use it any more.

— I don't believe you.

I sensed he was afraid. He fidgeted, moving from foot to foot. I tried to smile to show him I wasn't cross.

— Yesterday you picked up the seagulls. The other days I saw your dog running around on the beach. He's fast. One day he'll catch one.

I liked the way the kid spoke. He reminded me of myself.

— Ah, you like dogs. You're one of the good guys, then?

Joël asked:

— Where did the dog come from, by the way?

I said and did exactly what I had said I would say and do if anyone bothered me with such a question.

Joël listened and responded:

— He can't have swum from the coast. Perhaps he came on a raft. I saw that once, in my early days at the lighthouse. A cat on a raft. Kids messing about.

Damien seemed to get over his shyness.

— Dad… the other night, Monsieur Lefayen was out in his boat.

Joël replied on my behalf, as if covering for me.

— I've done that myself, gone out for a paddle in the moonlight. This fucking lighthouse, there's no telling what it'll make you do next.

Suddenly, the kid became excited. He spoke loudly, confidently, and rolled his big old eyes.

— Dad, he was rowing dead fast. He was…

Joël directed a kick at his son's backside, but didn't connect.

— Listen to you, knowing everyone's business. Put a sock in it.

When we were eating, I asked Joël if he'd seen the police again and he seemed surprised.

— It's not like I'm inviting them over for fish chowder.

Why should I believe him? He's already kept things from me, and not little things. One, two, three, four things, I counted in my head. Plus the kid. Three men, a blind person and a kid. Two strapping lads, an upstart, a disabled person and a simpleton. I had to stop myself looking at my cleaver, which I knew was hanging up, just like a regular cleaver, above the tap.

As if it were a random observation, Joël said:

— By the way, did you know the coastguard is on the lookout for some Spanish smugglers who are meant to be hanging around?

— Smugglers?

— Drugs.

One of the guys spoke into his moustache:

— Apparently some connection with the trainees who were here before you.

I remained silent, to show my lack of concern. I had my nose in the trough.

— Any thoughts? Joël asked.

— Why should I have? I replied, getting up suddenly and moving quickly towards the sink. I placed my hands on the cold stoneware of the draining board, as if I were in the pulpit about to give a sermon. My eyes alighted on the cleaver, its blade marked with a thousand tiny shiny marks showing its use. I filled my lungs with air, to bursting point, then expelled it very slowly.

— All right, Geoffroy? Joël said. You've gone very quiet.

That's nothing new, as Joël knows very well. Joël's eyes, being almost no use to him, are no longer on his face but in his belly, and they see better than before.

— I'm fine, I said.

Then I bent down. I took in another lungful of air and let it out slowly, like before, and I opened the cupboard under the sink and took out a half-bottle of brandy.

I slammed it down on the table.

— Monkey brandy, I said.

And I told the story.

— Well, it's good brandy! What did you do with the creature?

I had to introduce them to Sheeta. Their eyes opened wide like children's, even Joël's, behind his pince-nez. Damien was clinging to his father's side.

While waiting for the tide we passed the time joking about Sheeta and knocking back the brandy. Before leaving, Joël, by now distinctly merry, gave me a great big slap on the back.

— The worst of it is over. The weather will get better from here on. You'll have earned a good long rest afterwards. I'm not joking, Geoffroy, I don't know if I've ever seen you in such a good mood.

It's true I've got good reason to be in a good mood, after mourning for my seagull and the slaughter of the birds: Lise has agreed to marry me.

This must be what happiness is. A sense of calm you feel in every inch of your body. The sense that you are, after all, a little bit like everyone else, even that you might be among the fortunate few.

She's due at the lighthouse in two days.

A wife, a dog. Friends. Who knows, perhaps, tomorrow, a family?

Cold

I sensed Lise's nervousness on the phone. Her voice was staccato and her instructions bizarre.

So what if she's killed her husband? I can't see that upsetting many people, that a guy who poisons the life of his wife should be removed from the surface of the Earth. Twenty people at most, three quarters of whom will have forgotten after a fortnight, with the remaining quarter being the next to go.

Killing isn't so terrible. Dying may be, but killing…

This evening I regret not killing Joël, Damien and the supply team.

It's all Lise's fault. Lise has turned my brain to mush, like a crust of bread left in milk.

I'm going to try to pull myself together.

I spent the morning preparing the bridal suite (the engineer's room).

I collected shells from the beach, seaweed, a dozen dead seagulls and starfish. I strung up fishing nets on the walls, with plenty of slack. You see that sometimes in restaurants. I've always liked it. Then I affixed three birds to the wall (some nailed through the neck, others at the wing tips) and sprinkled the rest of the room with shells, seagulls and starfish as fancy took me. As a final touch I placed a few glass eyes here and there and, I must say, I'm proud of this idea, because it really worked. If Lise doesn't like it, I'll remove them. I'm a bit worried about the smell, from the starfish. When they dry, they stink, like intestines. I don't care. But a woman…

I had a bit of time for finishing touches. I went

to get my mallard and hung it above our bed. It's my wedding gift to Lise. I hope she'll like it.

Katleen and Steeven also benefited from my burst of creativity. I made them some lovely costumes from hessian sacks and adorned them with necklaces, bracelets and anklets of shells and feathers.

I'm nervous. Tomorrow is the big day. In less than an hour you'll be in my arms. I may find myself lost for words.

I fiddle with the rings that I have woven out of wire. I put them in my mouth and spit them out.

The fridge is crammed with food. Joël has been great. We're going to have a feast. Afterwards, hopefully, there'll be dancing.

Morning, pink sky and light wind

As I write, my wife is asleep. Occasionally I interrupt the writing of my diary to look at her. She's so beautiful! The fire in the chimney creates orange reflections in her orange hair.

Lise got a bit tired towards the end. But mostly she was amazing.

She arrived yesterday, I think, standing up in her rubber dinghy, astride the waves like a creature of the sea, or a member of a superior race, a sort of Amazonian goddess. It was dark, but I saw her all the same, perhaps thanks to her flaming-red hair and the bright orange gear.

Lise was able to beach the dinghy. I helped her to unload the diving gear, the tanks and wetsuits, and, as agreed on the phone, I scuttled the boat.

Yes, I scuttled the dinghy.

I definitely sensed that Bambi was a bit jealous when I kissed Lise. But he'll get over it.

Lise didn't wait for my permission to start getting drunk. The 'monkey brandy' did the job.

I'm getting to know her. When she's drunk, she's unrefined and wants instant satisfaction. Which is what I gave her in the kitchen, against the sink, right in front of my cleaver. I love, above all, the manner in which she parts her thighs. Like a contortionist from the Peking Circus. While this is going on, if I hold and lift her breasts, I catch sight of a frizz of hair at her groin. This glimpse, without fail, causes me to lose control. And as Lise says 'Shit' every time this happens, I have to get going again.

I introduced our guests with genuine innocence tinged with a kind of restrained frenzy, like a cat that drops a bloody mouse at the feet of its mistress. Alcohol played a part in Lise's getting to know Katleen and Steeven, as she didn't seem at all surprised. She simply said hello. In truth, her mouth gave nothing away and her eyes were two holes filled with milky agate. What's important is she didn't turn and run.

Alcohol was also no doubt behind her reaction to the bridal suite – 'I love it' – without batting an eyelid. She didn't even appear to mind the smell.

Towards midnight, my head was hurting so badly it was like someone had inserted a 12-gauge needle into my ear. And then, suddenly, it went, allowing me to go up to the lantern with Bambi. I wanted to have a sense of the vast world outside and to give thanks for the great happiness that had come upon me. But several seagulls were dying silently up there, like invalids dragged from their armchairs and beds by some unknown sadist. I did an about-turn and pounced on a cockroach that had no place there in this moment of joy and celebration.

I slept like the dead.

Lise woke me. She was already drunk.

She said, in a panic, her eyes wide and her voice broken and grimly serious:

— The lighthouse!

— What about it?

— Have you seen the time?

It was gone nine o'clock.

— Fuck!

I jumped up, but Lise let out a laugh that was all teeth and gums. Then she took my hand.

— Don't worry. I put it out.

I breathed out. She'd got me. I laughed as well. It was a long time since I'd laughed. I'm not sure if I'd ever laughed.

However, I stopped laughing as abruptly as if the sky had suddenly darkened with warplanes. Lise might have been my betrothed, but she had just played a dirty trick on me. I stared at her with my eyes so wide it started to hurt and I beat my fist with all my force on the frame of the sleigh bed. In my head a voice was saying: 'Your knives are in the box at the end of the bed.' I closed my eyes as forcefully as I'd opened them, then swooped down on my box and grabbed a balsa saw with a blade as fine as cheese wire.

My eyes, this time, were not hurting, but I looked deeply into Lise's.

She approached me, apparently without fear, one strap of her nightdress having fallen off her shoulder. One of her breasts had fallen free and begun to rock gently with the swaying of her hips as she walked. She took the saw out of my hand, put it down on the pedestal table, made me sit down in the armchair, twisted her mouth and licked my cheek, saying, 'I'm your little fucking Bambi on heat.' When she turned round and stuck her arse in the air, wiggling it like she was in a peep show, I forgot everything else and did what I had to do.

Lise put on the same outfit as yesterday. It worked for me, the bizarre orange for a bizarre wedding. I put on a clean shirt and marked the occasion with a squirt of lavender water on my chest.

We entered the chapel to *Jesu, Joy of Man's Desiring* hissing out of a knackered tape recorder intended for the tourists. They were all there: our witnesses Katleen and Steeven, my little conger eel on the wall, Sheeta, in the role of priest, my stuffed crayfish and some of my farmed crayfish that I had released the day before into the chapel, my one-eyed bear, Bambi of course, and even the sun, streaming through the windows.

Throughout the service, apart from when the priest handed us the rings, Lise kept her left hand on the mallard and her right hand on my cock, which became softer and harder according to her caresses. The extraordinary spectacle was transformed instantly into a delicious memory, partly due to exhaustion, but also because I promptly fucked my wife up against the oculus in front of everyone, in front of these kind and well-mannered guests, who acted like it was the most normal thing in the world.

All that was missing was a shower of rice on our blessed heads and delighted smiles. I was happy this morning, I am happy this evening. This marriage has made me complete. It was about time.

There was, however, a fly in the ointment. Beyond the doors, the spoilsports were gathering. Monsieur Rouleau, my father, the two Rogers, to name but a few. If they had closed the door, that would have been something, but they nattered up their sleeves and stifled unseemly laughter. One of them even burst out laughing. Otherwise they whispered my name, 'Geoffroy, Geoffroy, Geoffroy.' The syllables merging to the point where it made me half-mad. The voices reached me as if carried by diseased smoke to my ears. I turned around and I saw them, with their dirty teeth, their bruised eyes, their mocking smiles that tore apart their faces. Furious, I left my prie-dieu and went to deal with them, upsetting a few chairs on my way, but the cowards had disappeared. As I hammered at the walls with my fists and shouted, 'Bunch of bastards, I'll kill you all,' Lise, beautiful Lise, whose sweet breath smelt like a Christmas chocolate liqueur, took my head in her hands and said, kissing me on the forehead and in the very next moment kneading my cock, 'It's over, it's over. Come on. Let's fuck.'

Dark night

— Why did you lie, Monsieur Lefayen?

Jacques arrived towards the end of the morning with the high tide, accompanied by a uniformed cop. The short time that passed between the moment when Lise and I spotted the police launch and their stepping inside the lighthouse was just enough to get Katleen and Steeven under salt, chuck all my embalming kit and products on top of the ring, hurriedly clear the engineer's room, muzzle Bambi and shut him in, and above all get Lise equipped so she could hide in one of the rainwater tanks.

I didn't answer right away. I was fascinated by his hands. A doctor's hands, with tufts of white hair and long fingers ending in nails with perfect half-moons.

His face is beautiful as well. His eyes are soft and imposing at the same time, very bright under bushy eyebrows like circumflexes. He has lovely salt-

and-pepper hair, combed back. He looks terribly intelligent.

He was looking at me with a degree of sympathy, like a schoolmaster might regard his star pupil who, for once, has let himself down.

— I was afraid I might get into trouble.

I was considerably taller than him and broader, too. As for the sidekick, with his pathetic little traffic policeman's cap, I could have fossilised him in the wall with a single cough. But I remained sitting down, my knees pressed together, incapable of lifting a little finger.

Jacques had recently learnt that Steeven, on the day of his visit to Cordouan with Katleen, had telephoned a local photographer from his mobile. The photographer had asked what it was about and Steeven had explained that they were in the area, he and his wife-to-be. This crazy Englishman wanted to know six months in advance what the fellow would charge for an evening wedding at the lighthouse.

Jacques walked slowly up and down. I sensed that he still had more.

— Lise Tricoul disappeared four days ago.

— It's true that I no longer seem to get her on the radio.

Jacques studied his fingernails.

— She set fire to her house. It went up in smoke. They found the bodies of her husband and daughter. The daughter was identified by her jewellery. For her father it was a matter of dental records. They must have been tied up.

— How do they know it was Lise who killed them?

— Did I say it was, Monsieur Lefayen? No one knows. But one is bound to ask why she disappeared the same day.

This news cheered me up more than it concerned me. It meant they weren't listening in. It also meant their surveillance of the lighthouse was no more sophisticated than a kid's telescope. If not, they'd have already been and picked up Lise. Unless all this was part of a strategy beyond my understanding.

Jacques's approach was one of the gentlest menace.

— Monsieur Lefayen, I wonder if you're protecting Lise?

I'd no doubt reacted too quickly when he'd said she'd set fire to her home.

There was a way to get out of that.

— I can't deny the engineer brightened up my day. She's the first woman I've seen in three months. Do you know what I mean? I wouldn't like to think she's mixed up in anything like this.

Jacques grabbed a chair and leaned in closer. He looked at my hands, which still bore the scars from my unfortunate performance of the other day, with the lantern, as well as more recent scratches. I tensed up. I imagined he was going to try the same tactic as he had used on the phone, which I would not be able to resist for very long. He sent the uniform off to have a look around.

— I know you weren't feeling too good a little while ago.

— I'm better now.

The remains of the bruising on my brow triggered no questions. Jacques is interested in more serious matters.

— I'm sorry to ask this, but tell me about your relationships with women.

He's almost like a sorcerer this guy. I should have just said, 'Everything's fine in that department,' but instead, for some reason, I said:

— I don't have any.

— Since when?

— Since always.

— Never?

I looked down.

— Only with professionals.

Jacques liked me, I was sure of it. Or he was winding me up.

— What about Lise Tricoul? Your relationship with her.

He had me in a hold. Somehow I managed to wriggle free.

— I find her attractive. That's as far as it goes.

Jacques seemed frustrated. He questioned me further about Lise, and about the English couple, and then he made me repeat everything. I got a little bit muddled up, but I think I put up an honourable resistance.

A moment later, the uniform returned saying, 'I found this.' By 'this' he meant Sheeta and Bambi. Sheeta was still wearing the priest's stole that I had draped on her shoulders for the ceremony. In the open air and in daylight, this pantomime struck me as somewhat pathetic.

The uniform let go of Bambi, who charged at me, his big brush of a tail wagging like crazy. I removed his muzzle.

— There are crayfish in the chapel and up the stairs.

Jacques looked at me intensely, this time with an expression like a teacher disconcerted by a problem kid.

— You've been here since the start of October, is that right?

To be honest, I can't remember how long I've been in this bloody lighthouse. Nevertheless, I said, 'Yes, that's right.'

Jacques stroked Bambi.

— If we hadn't found him, we'd have been accusing you of killing him. A beautiful animal, in apparent good health, who loves to run after seagulls on the beach. Why deprive us of his company when we come to pay you a little visit?

True, it was stupid to have hidden him. I'd panicked.

The uniform continued to deliver his report:

— There are cellars, but the door's locked.

Jacques picked up Sheeta by her arm with a look of disgust.

— Don't tell me you stuffed a monkey.

I told him about the barrel. Jacques picked at the stole.

— What about this?

— That's just me amusing myself.

The uniform rummaged in his pocket and pulled out a pair of tights.

— I found them in the room with the fireplace, where it stinks, by the way.

He meant the engineer's room.

— Let's go, said Jacques, depositing Sheeta on a coil of rope.

The fishing nets were still hung on the walls and, here and there, were a few white feathers and the odd trace of blood. There was a smell of vomit.

Jacques was fiddling with the tights.

— I'd say there's a dead rat under a piece of furniture, Geoffroy.

Geoffroy... He had just called me by my Christian name. How good my Christian name sounded in his mouth.

— I started work on a fish a couple of days ago. I didn't use enough borax and it didn't dry out correctly. I threw it away a bit ago. I'll open a window.

Jacques didn't reply. He approached my toolbox, squatted down, had a look at it, then got up, remaining silent. He wound Lise's tights around his hand, as he might do if he were nervous. Then he spoke.

— She must have forgotten them the last time she was here...

— Yes.

— I'll bet I took the words right out of your mouth, eh, Monsieur Lefayen?

We left the room, Jacques with Lise's mallard in his hands.

— Your latest creation?

— Yes.

— Nice.

I nodded in acknowledgement.

Jacques was noticeably a lot more tense than he had been earlier.

He asked me to show him the way to the chapel. He made no mention of the crayfish. Only the conger eel caught his eye.

— Without question, Geoffroy, you've got magic fingers.

I felt myself turning red.

— I agree the work looks good, especially in the chapel.

Bambi had followed us. Jacques, who was looking at the stained-glass window featuring St Peter, then at the one featuring St Anne, spoke without turning his head.

— Could you explain how this dog ended up at Cordouan?

I told him about Joël, the cat tied to a life raft by some kids. Jacques kept his mouth shut. Apparently he didn't know about the smugglers, or he was holding on to that for later. He took out a mobile phone and asked someone to check if, among Lise's entourage, there might have been a red setter answering to the name of…

— What's his name, Monsieur Lefayen?

— Bambi.

Jacques called Bambi. Bambi turned his head.

— Bambi. Or any name. Could be called Pluto for all I know.

It's interesting to see how a man can feel strong with a phone next to his ear, a colleague to hand, the penal code in his pocket and, up his sleeve, the Minister of the Interior, and even the armed forces if necessary. When in fact he owes his life to nothing more than the 'good doggie' side of his character and the fatherly look in his eye. Also to the banging headache I've had throughout this interview, during which I've forced myself to give brief answers, in order to keep to a minimum the amount of trouble I land myself in.

But I was also aware that if I killed Jacques, and his underling as a bonus, the time remaining that I could spend with Lise would be even shorter.

Jacques didn't leave. Suddenly – how could I have forgotten it? – the image of Lise floating in the rainwater tank, her mouth deformed by the regulator, passed before my eyes. Believing her to be on her second bottle (wrongly, as she had been able to slide under the *Poussée d'Archimède* and roll herself up in a tarpaulin after the uniform had been by), I kept looking at my watch every couple of minutes.

— Are you expecting someone, Geoffroy?

— I just need to call the subdivision.

— We'll let you get on.

I breathed out.

But Jacques wanted to see the log. He gave it a skim-read.

— After the sixth you no longer made a note of the date?

— I need to bring it up to date.

— And your handwriting seems unsteady.

— That's because of my hand. I hurt myself mending the boiler.

He carried on looking at it for a few more minutes, then closed it without a word.

He had to have a look at the cellar. Luckily, it

hadn't smelt bad for some time. I opened up and anticipated his questions.

— It's the ammoniated salt. Some work was done, last winter. The workmen left it there. I've not touched it.

The bags of cement and lime, the shovels and the wheelbarrow lent my story a certain credibility.

— I would have sworn it was to dry your fish for stuffing.

Jacques didn't insist. He took a bit of salt between his fingers, sniffed it, tasted it and spat it out. He asked the uniform to fill a little container he found in his pocket.

I thought that this time they were finally going to leave me in peace, especially since the tide was on my side, but Jacques wanted to go up to the lantern. Once up there he placed his beautiful doctor's hands on the guardrail, looking back towards Royan.

— Great view.

Especially since it was a clear day.

He took a book from the inside pocket of his coat.

— Do you read, Geoffroy?

— Before, yes, a bit.

— What did you read, before?

— Adventure stories. Also Zola, Victor Hugo.

— Do you know Scott Fitzgerald?

— No.

Jacques turned to the uniform, who had followed us with the same loyalty as Bambi.

— What about you, Baptiste? Do you know Scott Fitzgerald?

— No, Monsieur.

— Funny old thing, life, Jacques continued. I picked this book at random and took it out of the library at Verdon last week. It's a biography of Scott Fitzgerald. This morning, in the launch coming to the lighthouse, I read a passage I liked very much. I'll read it to you, Geoffroy.

Jacques flicked through his book, from the back, frowning.

— Here we are: 'How strange to have failed as a social creature – even criminals do not fail that way – they are the law's "Loyal Opposition", so to speak. But the insane are always mere guests on earth, eternal strangers carrying around broken decalogues that they cannot read.'

He closed the book and looked at me.

I didn't say anything. I felt a strong need to piss.

Jacques regarded the horizon once more, towards Verdon this time.

— How many lives have been saved thanks to you, Geoffroy?

— I don't know. It's difficult to work out.

— Hundreds, thousands…

— Without the lighthouse, there could have been any number of accidents and shipwrecks.

— And, more importantly, without guys like you to keep watch.

— For sure…

— That's right, Geoffroy, that's right. I don't know a single judge who wouldn't take that into account.

Winter

How much time is Jacques going to give us? There's so much for us still to do, me and Lise.

Since Jacques left we haven't wasted a minute. The first thing I did was give Lise a refresher course in how to read clouds. She had forgotten. Today, for example, the whitish, fibrous veil of cirrostratus announces bad weather. If the filaments had been longer, there would have been less to worry about.

On an empty stomach, Lise is a different person. The sky fascinates her. The names of the clouds, just for starters, she finds attractive. Altostratus, cumulonimbus… I had to repeat them to her at least twenty times.

We made love, of course, but not like usual. It was softer, more like dancing. Lise blinked slowly while we were doing it, like a broken doll being laid down. Rather than clinging painfully to me, it was like she was flying in love, or swimming. She was fluid and beautiful.

Then I performed my baptismal dive, in four metres of water, in a natural well just off shore. Lise held my hand. Ballasted with all the gear, I simply blocked my nose to equalise the pressure. Then we fluttered in slow motion for five or six minutes that felt like hours. It was good. So was the sun afterwards, on our invigorated bodies.

Lise complimented me. I'm at ease in the water, like a fish. Yes, a fish. That's what I would have liked to have been. Especially since at the bottom of that great well, there were some extraordinary fish: shoals of damselfish wriggling like tiny bells among the Gorgon-like seaweed, coral-grazing parrotfish, flocks of pennant coralfish. But we also saw the nasty moray eel and the shadow of the enormous hump-head wrasse, the size of a bus. And a thousand other tiny creatures that eventually required us to resurface because my head was beginning to thump.

I don't remember very much after the dive. I probably slept and I must have injured myself during sleep because I woke up with my forearms bandaged and painful.

Lise is asleep. How right she was just now! I wanted to get Katleen and Steeven kitted up to dive with us tomorrow, but that's stupid. You have to be able to swim to dive and Katleen and Steeven don't look to me like they're able to swim. They'd be better off up there hanging from the cornice where I hung the two Spanish smugglers the other day. I'm not worried: I'm sure they can look after themselves.

I'm going to go and rejoin Lise and watch her sleep. Well, with one eye, since I've just blinded myself in my left eye. Why? Because one eye is sufficient. The other I give to Joël and to those who don't see well at night.

I did it with one of my knives. It made a right funny old noise. *Fluntz*, or something like that. There was no pain. I didn't feel anything, I swear.

I could even die and feel no pain.

One day

It's hardly a comfortable position, but it beats being locked up. Leaning against the base of the lighthouse, a strong smell of fuel in my nostrils. It's under the fingernails on my left hand, even under my scalp (I've made incisions in order to fill myself with petrol). Everything up to ten metres around me smells of it as well, the *Poussée d'Archimède*, my fishing rods, the lantern covers, which I've dragged down from up above, the pulleys from the dip net, the dip net itself, the rope, my waders, and finally my bear, my lovely big old one-eyed bear, the only souvenir I have of my father (my father bought it for my brother, who didn't need it where he was going).

Lise is sleeping the eternal sleep, her head against my shoulder. The fire will wake her, though. As for Bambi… 'Bambi, Bambi… Good dog, good dog.' He's there, moaning away. This morning I wanted to cut his paws off with my adze, to turn him into a fish like me, but at the last moment remembered that Bambi's not a fish. Bambi's a cocker spaniel mongrel whose tail no one has bothered to dock. I put this right.

My journal is propped up against my right knee. I write very well since losing an eye. I feel I get to the heart of things. My diary is perhaps the only thing that will remain of the lighthouse, as my plan is to stick it in a tin that should resist the flames. It's a biscuit tin that I've painted black, like a black box in an aeroplane. I'd like people to know my story. It's not that it's better than any other lighthouse keeper's, but it could be of interest to artists. Taxidermists, perhaps. Or those with a love of Egyptian art (I must say if I hadn't decided to burn down Cordouan, I would have been proud to see the mummies of Katleen and Steeven in a museum, alongside those of my conger eel, mallard and crayfish).

I think about good old Jacques. Where would I be without him? I owe him everything. He cured me, with his doctor's hands. And to think that I considered killing him!

As for Lise, I swear that it happened as I'm about to relate: she did it all on her own. This morning we were twenty or thirty metres down, in the big blue. She pulled out her regulator like it was a normal thing to do. Then she started swimming like a seahorse, or a lion, and she must have died, because once she reached the surface, her distended body reminded me of that of my little blackbird Geoffroy. When I think about it, twenty metres doesn't sound that deep.

Maybe it was thirty. In fact I think we were at least a hundred metres down. The well had got a lot deeper since yesterday, like a kind of oubliette. We were at five hundred metres, at least, among the deep-sea fish with enormous phosphorescent eyes. Yes, that's it. And Lise climbed too quickly, foolishly. She didn't stop to decompress. When I'm burnt to a crisp, when my nails and scalp are nothing but ash, I will be her decompression chamber. She'll stay there a week, eat there, sleep there, perhaps make love with two or three woodlice there, and afterwards she'll be able to cavort in the grass. I owe that to Lise, the only woman I've ever loved. I love her still. I'll always love her.

It's her, indirectly, who gave me the idea of burning down Cordouan. When Jacques told me that Lise had set the fire at her place, that reminded me of something: before getting themselves picked up by the police, the two Rogers had tried to set fire to their boat. But as I write that, I'm no longer sure. Perhaps it was me who wanted to burn *La Geneviève*. In any case, fire follows me, so let it catch up with me. I'll purify myself in the flames of the great Cordouan. Fire smells clean, as clean as a mountain spring. I'm going to set fire to the fire that is the lantern, which will explode like an atomic bomb and cleanse the entire area, wiping the slate clean, from the men on the coast to the poor health of my mother. It will give life back to the seagulls struck down by unknown hand. The smoke will form a long finger pointing to the sky, as silent and straight as a cobra, and in the lighthouse transformed into altocumulus, foretelling a clear spell, I will see, finally, the face of my Cyclops father.

But first there will be a young fire, a lively fire, a fire of joy that no fire hose will be able to put out, and even if the sea could rise up to extinguish it, it would reignite. Too bad if ships collide and oil tankers run aground on the beaches like whales. Cordouan will not have resisted the flames of King Geoffroy, the one-eyed king who burns with love for the whole world, the one-eyed king who had a wife, two friends and a dog.

I hear a megaphone. I recognise the warm voice of Jacques. Now Joël. 'Don't be a fool' – is that what Joël's saying? Eh? What an idea! There's no danger of me being a fool! As if that's what's going on! I'm too attached to life for that. And I'm frightened of being thrown in a cell for the rest of my days. Don't worry, Joël. I'm just going to strike a little match. Someone's knocking on the postern, down below. It's Joël and the doctor from before. Stop! They're doing my head in. What's this helicopter buzzing over the lighthouse like a great big fly? There must be someone drowning! My God! I hope Katleen and Steeven haven't done anything silly!

I'll get the Spaniard's gun out anyway, in case the chopper is only hanging round to annoy me.

There's Jacques's voice again, and Joël's, both of them distorted by the swell. It's good to hear their voices. Thank you, my friends, for coming to say hello. Or goodbye, yes, goodbye, which amounts to the same thing. Thank you for being there to hear my last words, which will be those of a dog that's been beaten all his life. I don't want tears. I'll just say I feel like barking. Look, I'm going to bark. There we are.

I just barked. Woof, woof. Bambi is back, without his tail. Joël? Do you want me to light your pipe, Joël? I can do you this final favour, since you, too, have been good to me. Where's my lighter? I must have left it in the kitchen. I'll go and look for it just as soon as the crayfish have stopped nibbling my legs. My eye hurts. There might be some little creatures poking about in there as well. What's this? Now my hands are bleeding. I must have cut myself with the bread knife. Or maybe that happened yesterday. It's not just my hands. My whole body is bleeding and yawning in the open air under the Cordouan sky. Let them stuff me! Let them stuff me! What have I gone and done? I'm bleeding from everywhere, like Jesus on the cross. Do you need to see any more to know how much I suffer?

Geoffroy Lefayen, the so-called executioner of Cordouan, was shot by
officers from the elite tactical unit
of the Gendarmerie Nationale at
15.00 hours on 14 January 1993.
His diary has been retranscribed
as it was found, with the exception
of the last few pages, which were
indecipherable.

Afterword

The same day I finished reading *Pharricide*, I happened to read D.H. Lawrence's 'The Man Who
Loved Islands' and was struck by an interesting
affinity between these two studies of self-imposed
isolation. In de Swarte's novel, Geoffroy Lefayen
has accepted a position as lighthouse keeper at
Cordouan: '"I'll do it. Without a colleague. Without
trainees."' In Lawrence's story, Mr Cathcart has
been inhabiting increasingly small islands until he is
living alone on 'just a few acres of rock'. Both men,
at the same time as distancing themselves from soci-
ety, express a kind of existential horror: Geoffroy is
frightened of his own name, and Mr Cathcart finds
reading his name on an envelope repulsive.

Geoffroy, living in the shadow of his stillborn
brother, has difficulty forming lasting relationships:
his mother is 'in the nuthouse' and he hasn't seen

her for years; he has never seen his father, who entered a monastery before Geoffroy was born; his few
friends have lost touch, are in prison or dead, apart
from the blinded Joël. Where Mr Cathcart expe-
riences a falling-away of identity, Geoffroy is keen
to define himself. Early in the novel, Geoffroy tells
us that he is kind – 'I feel it warming me from inside, this kindness. It feels solid, if naive' – but, as he
elaborates, this assertion of kindness warps into an
image of himself as a 'half-crazed' dog, 'panting in
a panic', who 'would happily accept being sent back
to my kennel with a sharp word or a slap for being
a nuisance'.

Later, he depicts himself as 'a dog that's been
beaten all his life'. The implication is that these
sharp words and slaps and beatings are his experience of human contact. He tos and fros between
pity and violence in a single line: 'I stayed until the
evening blubbing like a woman on the bed in the
watch room holding a threadbare one-eyed teddy
bear tightly enough to suffocate the poor thing.' He
tells us that he is highly thought of by others for 'my
willingness to take risks, my strong constitution and
my heroic physique'. We soon come to see the irony
in this list of his positive traits.

Like Mr Cathcart, who, on his final island, 'did
not want to be approached', Geoffroy prays 'to God
no one comes to the lighthouse during those six
months, no one at all' and when visitors do come
he sometimes refuses to meet them. But where Mr
Cathcart seems simply to have lost interest in human company, Geoffroy prefers to see no one only

'because I'm afraid I'll fail to be reasonable'. He readily personifies the lighthouse that he has been employed to tend. Early in the narrative, he implies its authority: 'The lighthouse pretty much let me sleep until five.' He blames the lighthouse for his mental state – 'Cordouan had been doing my head in since dawn. It had been driving me mad' – and for the murder he commits: 'You see what you've done. You see what you've done to me. You see what you've done to them.' In the personified lighthouse, we can perceive both his mother, whose mental illness Geoffroy fears, and his eternally absent father: at the end of the novel, when Geoffroy describes how the lighthouse will burn, he imagines that, in the lighthouse, he 'will see, finally, the face of my Cyclops father'.

When Lise refuses his marriage proposal, telling him, 'Being on your own is messing with your head,' Geoffroy attacks the lighthouse: 'I dug my nails into Cordouan. "Fucking lighthouse," I yelled, at a deafening volume, a thousand times.' He knifes the chapel walls: 'It felt like I was attacking a sibling. "Serves you right," I repeated over and over'. The sibling who comes to mind is his stillborn brother, though it might equally represent Geoffroy himself, whose feeling that 'I'm becoming the lighthouse' foreshadows his desire, at the end of the novel, to set himself alight, to burn.

Geoffroy, like the lighthouse, is isolated, and exposed to periods of turbulence. After a long period of working patiently on his conger eel, he tells us that he's 'had to gag myself to avoid howling, banging my head against a wardrobe... piercing my fore-arms with sharp, precise jabs from my number three knife, number ten blade'. A sentence that starts in tranquillity takes a chillingly menacing turn: 'I felt quite serene when I heard that the engineer from Lighthouses and Beacons was coming, because I know I'm going to kill him.' There are similar jux-tapositions in 'The Man Who Loved Islands', in which, within one short paragraph, we move from 'the island was so lovely' to 'Strange floods of pas-sion came over you, strange violent lusts and imag-inations of cruelty.' The switch from calm to squall might take us by surprise, but the warnings are there. De Swarte slips in words and phrases that are like distant rumbles of thunder, alerting us to approach-ing trouble. After days of quiet routine, Geoffroy tells us that there's 'the faintest trace of madness in the air. I've been checking my knives and equip-ment.' He keeps himself to himself, because he's afraid he'll 'be tempted'. The waves that surround the lighthouse are 'in the grip of the moon', imply-ing lunar madness, and 'The wind has been trying to unscrew the lighthouse since this morning.' It is as if the environment itself is responsible for the mental disturbance, which is also expressed in Lawrence's story: 'The Master himself began to be a little afraid of his island. He felt here strange violent feelings he had never felt before, and lustful desires that he had been quite free from.'

If Geoffroy's mood can turn bad like the weather, it can clear in just the same way. As with a stormy sea, 'By tomorrow you wouldn't know there'd been anything wrong'. After a violent fit, he is 'feeling full of love. I want to kiss the rocks, the silt, the crabs, the seagulls, my crayfish and the whole world.' His feeling, after Lise's acceptance of his marriage proposal, that 'This must be what happiness is. A sense of calm you feel in every inch of your body' is echoed in Lawrence's story: 'The islander said to himself: "Is this happiness?" He said to himself: "I am turned into a dream. I feel nothing, or I don't know what I feel. Yet it seems to me I am happy."'

Geoffroy leaves gaps in his account of events, so that, for example, there is no mention of the English couple prior to him telling us 'The English couple arrived this morning.' Following a couple of bizarre and abortive attempts to approach Lise sexually, Geoffroy is, as far as we know, having sex with her for the first time, when he informs us that 'I think the last time I fucked her she was out of it. Perhaps the last two times.' Things seem to happen beneath the surface or in darkness or out of our line of sight. It is disorienting for the reader, as if we have not been paying sufficient attention.

Geoffroy's statement that 'the dormant taxidermist inside' him has awakened and his musing on the stuffing of living creatures, 'whether it's a conger eel, a lion, or even you or me', immediately juxtaposed with 'The English couple arrived this morning' is wonderfully, hideously suggestive. Describing the English couple, he fixates on the woman's skin, her well-defined muscles, her beautiful veins. He finds her neck 'appetising'. We understand at this point what is likely to happen; the surprise – the morbid peak – is not that he kills but that he desires to bring what he has killed – the eel, the English couple – back to life. At first, this seems like a childlike failure to process what he has done, as if he could undo such a thing. His actions can appear contradictory: he maims a man, then fantasises about caring for him – 'Washing him, warming him up, going fishing for him, cooking for him, feeding him, monitoring his progress day by day' – and then finishes him off; on one page he says, 'I regret not killing Joël' and on the next he says, 'Joël has been great.'

In fact, though, there is not such a contradiction in this. For Geoffroy, killing someone can be an act of love. It is 'out of the kindness of his heart' that he murders the English couple, whom he likes. He is the Egyptian jackal god Anubis, granting eternal life, gifting them eternal love. Bringing them back to life involves stuffing them, after which he dresses and poses them so that they can be his Christmas Eve companions and the witnesses at his wedding. 'They're my friends, the English couple. Real friends who don't betray you.'

His love for his dog is expressed in the same horrific way: '"Bambi, Bambi... Good dog, good dog"... This morning I wanted to cut his paws off with my adze, to turn him into a fish like me'. There is a nasty irony in the fact that, as a lighthouse keeper, Geoffroy is a dedicated preserver of life: 'How many lives have been saved thanks to you, Geoffroy?' asks Jacques. 'Without the lighthouse, there could have been any number of accidents and shipwrecks.' Meanwhile, Geoffroy has been busy in the cellar, literally preserving people with salt and chemicals, so that they won't rot.

By the end of 'The Man Who Loved Islands', Mr Cathcart has lost interest in his work, in opening a book, in knowing the names of birds; he is irritated if 'the great silence' is broken, even by his own voice, and has 'ceased to register his own feelings... It was as if all life were drawing away... "Soon," he said to himself, "it will all be gone, and in all these regions nothing will be alive." He felt a cruel satisfaction in the thought.'

Having rejected life, he is left, at the end, on his bare hump of rock, beneath a sky that has 'mysteriously darkened and chilled', looking out at the 'stark' and 'lifeless' sea. *Pharricide* ends not only with Geoffroy's death but with Geoffroy's fantasy of destroying the lighthouse, yet even as he prepares to strike a match to set fire to himself, he is 'attached to life'; he 'burns with love for the whole world'. Like Mr Cathcart anticipating an end to 'all life', Geoffroy wants to 'cleanse the entire area, wiping the slate clean', but in contrast to Mr Cathcart's annihilistic impulse, Geoffroy's is almost humanitarian – he would be doing it for 'the men on the coast' and 'the poor health of my mother' and to 'give life back to the seagulls struck down by unknown hand'. Crucially, Geoffroy himself has put a knife into one of his eyes and cut into his flesh, in an echo of the way in which he prepares a body for stuffing, and now cries out, 'Let them stuff me! Let them stuff me!' We understand that, for Geoffroy, taxidermy is a life-giving act: 'if you stuff a living creature, death is not the end'. When he tells us that he is 'bleeding from everywhere, like Jesus on the cross', the comparison suggests his physical wounds and his feeling of having been abandoned by his father, but also a hope, perhaps, of resurrection. The bleak and brutal story of the executioner of Cordouan is, unexpectedly, an expression of his love of and desire for life.

Alison Moore

Acknowledgements

The translator wishes to thank John Saddler, Tim Shearer, Zoë McLean, Janet Penny, Julia Balcells, Anne de Swarte, Ros Sales, Patrick McGrath, Alison Moore, Alice Thompson, David Rose, Jean-Daniel Brèque, Gregory Norminton, Brian Radcliffe and P.V. Wolseley for their help and advice. P.V. Wolseley, in particular, was extremely generous with her time and expertise.

The typefaces used in this edition are Baskerville, designed by John Baskerville in the mid-eighteenth century, and Futura, designed by Paul Renner in 1927. It is printed on 90gsm Munken Premium at TJ International UK.

confingopublishing.uk